GREENGAGE HOLIDAY CHEER

Part two in the Greengage Series

EMMA STERNER-RADLEY

Heartsome Publishing

SIGN UP

Firstly, thank you for purchasing Greengage Holiday Cheer.

I frequently hold flash sales, competitions, giveaways and lots more.

To find out more about these great deals you will need to sign up to my mailing list by clicking on the link below:

http://tiny.cc/greengage

REVIEWS

I sincerely hope you will enjoy reading Greengage Holiday Cheer.

If you did, I would greatly appreciate a short review on your favourite book website.

Reviews are crucial for any author, and even just a line or two can make a huge difference

For Carol Hutchinson.

For her unwavering support, friendship and general badassery and adorableness.

ACKNOWLEDGMENTS

The first thank you goes to my wife, Amanda, for continuously promising me that I am indeed funny when I panic that no one will get my weird sense of humour.

Other thanks go to my editor Jessica Hatch and my proofreader Cheri Fuller. You are both unbelievably excellent at your jobs and a true joy to work with.

Thanks as always to my family for their patience and support. And to all the friends I neglect when I bury my head in a new book. You're the best for being there when I come back up for air!

And, as always;

In memory of
Malin Sterner
1973-2011
Jag saknar dig.

Chapter One

HOLIDAY CHEER

I t was the tenth of December on the small British island of Greengage. In a workman's cottage on the grounds of Howard Hall, the island's biggest manor house, Katherine "Kit" Sorel put her hands on her hips and sniffed the air. Now the cottage smelled of:

Cinnamon

Mulled Wine

Pine

An Open Fire

And Holiday Cheer.

At least that was what the packaging of the posh scented candles she'd just lit claimed. If you'd asked Kit what it smelled like, she'd say "Christmas." Or "Nice enough, I suppose" if you caught her when she was grumpy. She wasn't far off from 'grumpy' at the moment, but she was trying her best to aim for that holiday cheer that the candles promised.

As she was adjusting her glasses, some tinsel that had scrunched up on the sofa caught her eye. She picked it up and tossed it carelessly over the hearth. She'd decided a

Christmas tree was too much work for someone who wasn't in a Christmas mood, but supposed she had to decorate a bit. She'd settled on some tinsel over the fireplace and some scented candles. Oh, and an ugly Santa gnome thing, which probably belonged in the garden. That'd have to do for her first Christmas in the cottage she was renting from her girlfriend.

Kit's Christmas Grinchiness melted into the glow of love, probably complete with a stupid grin.

Girlfriend.

It still made her head swim that Laura Howard was her girlfriend. Greengage's favourite daughter, the successful businesswoman who was so passionate about her family's fruit farm, the caring sweetheart, the insatiable lover. All those things wrapped up in a package of big auburn curls, hazel eyes, freckles, rounded cheeks, and full lips. Oh, and amazing curves. Now that was the only package Kit wanted for Christmas. For once, it seemed her wishes would come true!

Kit's love glow faded again.

At least it will if Laura gets any time off from sorting out that bloody Christmas market. Damn the Greengage Events Committee for coming up with something to keep Laura so busy. Mabel and Ethel owe me.

The island's first ever Christmas market was to be arranged cheaply and at the last minute. It was the idea of two of Greengage's most famous troublemakers, who had just joined the events committee: the grumpy Mabel Baxter, aged seventy-eight, and the jovial Ethel Rosenthal, aged eighty. It was Ethel who had pushed Kit to buy a few Christmas decorations, despite Kit not wanting to celebrate Christmas at all this year. It didn't feel right. Especially not as she'd be celebrating alone.

Kit was relatively new to the island of Greengage, being a Londoner who'd been forced to move out in search of library work. The only blood relative she was in contact with was her father, and he was in Costa del Sol for the holidays with some new fling. Now, between the market and the launch of Gage Farm's new mulled wine, Laura was busy and might not have much time to celebrate the holidays with her. If she did get time to focus on Christmas, she'd probably feel compelled to celebrate it at Howard Hall with her bratty younger brother, since no one else wanted anything to do with him and Laura had a big, soft heart. Not even Kit's best friend would be with her for Christmas. Aimee and George, her toddler, were celebrating at their home in Southampton with some bloke Aimee had started dating.

Kit shoved her hands in her pockets and sighed when she realised that her boss at the library and adopted uncle-figure, Rajesh, wouldn't come over for Christmas, considering he was Hindu. Not that he kept to his religion much, but he did when it came to holidays. Kit suspected he might be using it as a convenient excuse to avoid socializing. Still, she'd miss him and his slobbering bulldog mix, Phyllis, who would surely have liked to knock over Kit's ugly Santa gnome and scarf down a slice of Christmas turkey.

No, it did not feel like a proper Christmas, so why should Kit have to decorate and pretend to be filled with holiday cheer?

That was exactly what she had said to Ethel when she ran into her by the town square a few days ago. Ethel had poked a bony finger into Kit's shoulder and chirped that traditions were important.

Kit was pretty sure she hadn't pouted. She was thirty

years old. She didn't pout. She had, however, whinged like a five-year-old not allowed chocolate.

"Ethel," she'd whimpered. "I don't want to decorate, listen to Christmas music, cook, and all that. It doesn't feel like Christmas. Why go through the motions? What's the point? You and Rajesh don't have to."

"No, but I celebrate Hanukkah. And Rajesh doesn't really celebrate things, Hindu or not. He's not a good example for you, walking around cursing ugly Christmas lights and looking like the Grinch after a long bath to get rid of the green."

"And the furriness."

Ethel shook her head. "Oh, dear bubeleh. Handsome as he is, we both know Rajesh Singh is furrier than even that… unique dog of his."

Kit could only shrug at the truth of this statement. Then Ethel had led her into a shop and over to the Christmas aisle. She made her buy the tinsel, the candles, and, yes, even the Santa gnome thingy which she had proclaimed "a precious little chap". The misshapen, bug-eyed little statue was staring at Kit right now, berating her for not having bought him any friends.

"Look, mate, you're supposed to bring me holiday cheer, so don't give me that look, or I'll plonk you out in the weeds in the garden," Kit growled at him. Then she went to the kitchen to make tea for one, grumbling about how much she hated living alone.

She stopped her hand before it had time to get out a mug for the tea. She stared at the green-glass bottle on the counter. Perhaps she should have a glass of Gage Farm's greengage mulled wine instead. After all, it was as much to blame for Laura's absence in her life as the Christmas market. Kit might as well get her revenge on the bottle by drinking it dry. It would also give her a reason to text Laura and let her know if she liked the mulled wine or not. Sure, she had promised to leave her girlfriend alone with her paperwork regarding the Christmas market, but Laura, being a sweetheart deeply in love with Kit, wouldn't refuse her a quick phone call.

A little bit merrier at that thought, Kit poured herself a full glass of the mulled wine. She returned to the living room with the glass in one hand and a book in the other, fully prepared to drop the book the second she had finished the wine and had an excuse to call her girlfriend.

As she passed the Santa gnome, she muttered, "I don't care if you are my only company at the moment. You still don't get a glass, you ugly sod."

Chapter Two

THE THREE WISE GAY COUPLES

The next evening, Kit was on a barstool in Pub 42 watching the owners, Shannon and Rachel, bicker behind the bar. They'd been the first openly gay couple on the small and old-fashioned island of Greengage. The second had been the two blokes they owned this bar with, Matt and Josh. And the third, Kit was chuffed to say, was her and Laura. Three couples. That was it. Not enough for a Pride parade, but more than Kit had assumed there'd be when she first arrived last spring.

Sipping her Diet Pepsi, Kit tried not to eavesdrop on the women's conversation. Still, it was obvious that, as always, it was Rachel who was upset. She wore her heart on her sleeve and was very vocal if anyone scuffed up against it. In general, Shannon and Rachel were like a lot of May-December couples. The younger partner, Rach, who was about Kit's age, was the impetuous and passionate one while Shannon, who was somewhere in her late forties, was more patient and willing to compromise. Kit saw Shannon place her hand on her short afro and blow out a long breath, something that only seemed to infuriate Rachel further.

Rachel turned to Kit, clearly seeking support. "I'm right, aren't I?"

Kit squirmed. "Uh, I wasn't listening. I was busy looking at you and thinking what a cute couple you are."

"Stop trying to cheer me up," Rachel snarled. "I'm pissed off because the three idiots I run this place with want to set up a drinks stall at the Christmas market. Like we aren't already worked off our feet here!"

Shannon held up her hands. "All we're saying is that it would be a great way to network and to find new customers. You know the older and more conservative islanders aren't sure about us. They find us intimidating because we're queer, and this place looks more like a restaurant than a classic old man's pub. This would be a form of outreach."

"An expensive and time-consuming one, babe. We have neither the extra funds nor the extra time," Rachel whinged.

Kit tapped her fingers against her glass, trying to suppress her tendency to get involved in people's business and fix things. It felt like she should stay out of this one.

"Seems everyone's getting involved with this Christmas market," Kit said, in hopes for a change of subject. "Even the volunteers at the library have been bugging me to let them sell our old stock there. I had to explain to them that Greengage Library was certainly not paying for a spot at the market. I've seen the prices of them."

"Exactly!" Rachel cried. "They're bloody expensive, Shannon! Kit should know, she's sleeping with the person who's taking the money for setting up in one of those log cabin thingies."

Shannon turned to Kit. "Are we actually buying some sort of log cabin? Why not just have tents with heaters?"

Kit shrugged. "They're wooden huts. Laura says the island's events committee wants a certain aesthetic. To make it cosy and pretty for the tourists we hope to attract."

"Also, heaters or no heaters, it's winter. You'd still freeze your arse off in a tent all day," Rachel muttered.

"Yeah, that, too," Kit agreed. "But mainly it's to make it look quaint. After all, the main reason for doing this is to steal the visitors from the other more tourist-friendly islands. Apparently, our mayor made a deal with the next island over's councillors to cheaply rent these log huts."

"Don't they need them?" Rachel asked.

Kit swallowed a mouthful of her cola. "No, they usually have a Christmas market, but they ran out of funds this year and cancelled it. They only declared it in mid-November, though, which is when Greengage's events committee heard about it and started pressuring Laura to arrange a market." She took her glasses off and rubbed the bridge of her nose before adding, "A market should be planned for months, not weeks. There are permits to get, sellers to herd, supplies to gather, and confusing regulations to follow. All of which has to be done to get the market up around the middle of December. Like Laura didn't have enough on her plate with the upkeep of a crumbling Edwardian manor, orchards, and the family company. Not to mention the launch of the mulled wine."

A man walked up to the bar and signalled that he was ready to order. Rachel went over to serve him while Shannon looked to Kit, her kind face suddenly downcast.

"Ah, mate, I'm sorry Laura's so busy. Oh, and I'm also

sorry you had to hear our little spat. Rachel is testy these days. About everything."

Kit sucked air through her teeth. "She's not feeling the holiday cheer, then? Maybe she and I should start a club."

Shannon gazed at her girlfriend, who was making small talk with the man she was handing a pint. Rachel started putting her ginger hair up in a ponytail while saying something that made the customer laugh. Despite the bartender's temper, Kit had rarely met someone as easy-going and likely to cheer people up as Rachel. Still, Kit saw from her body language that this was customer-service joviality, not the real deal.

Shannon sighed. "I'm not sure the holidays are the biggest problem. There's something a little more personal."

This time, Kit couldn't keep her interest in solving problems from breaking to the surface. She cared too much about these two not to offer help.

"Shannon," she began. "Tell me to mind my own business if you like, but… is it personal as in 'I can't talk about it' or personal as in 'I would like to chat it out with a friend'? Because if it's the latter, I obviously volunteer."

Shannon looked at her for a while, tapping her fingers against the bar. "Well, if you're sure you don't mind getting involved?"

"Not at all. It'd be nice to have a project to stop me brooding on missing Laura and possibly being alone for Christmas. Besides, you guys helped Laura and me get together. I'd like to return the favour in some small way."

Shannon looked around the pub and then leaned over the bar so her face was a hair's breadth away from Kit's. "All right, but it's not something I can discuss here and now. Can I call you later?"

Kit was going cross-eyed at how close the other

woman suddenly was. In a theatrical whisper she replied, "Sure. Or we can meet at midnight in an abandoned alley and say the code phrase 'the sapphic ducks fly low in autumn' or something?"

Shannon stood back and frowned. "Kit, I'm being serious."

"Yeah, of course. I'm sorry. Call me whenever."

Shannon gave a curt nod. She squinted at Kit and said, "Don't take this the wrong way, mate. You know I think you're a good-looking woman, but might it be time for a haircut? I mean, I know the pain of maintaining short hair. Being butch isn't as low maintenance as people think. Although, you're more like *soft* butch." She surveyed Kit. "Like a lambswool kind of butch. Or a cottontail butch?"

Kit didn't get involved in the label banter. Instead she ran her hand through her pixie-cut black hair. Yes, it was getting wispy at the back and sticking out at odd angles.

Well, that's embarrassing. Thank goodness someone told me.

Kit sighed at yet another sign that she hadn't seen her girlfriend enough. Laura would've subtly mentioned that right away, just as she always pointed out when Kit's normally quite pink cheeks were redder than usual, making it sound like the sweetest compliment.

Or when she tells me that my glasses are smudged and takes them off, wipes them, then oh-so gently puts them on me, and says, "There. Can you see me now, dearest?"

Kit was getting choked up, which was bloody ridiculous and not dignified at all.

She collected herself and stood up. "Yeah, you're right. I'll book a hair appointment. Thanks for that and for the drink. I'm gonna go hunt down Laura. Busy as she is, I need to talk to her."

Shannon gave her a knowing smile. "Of course you do. Go make her take a break and kiss her dizzy. Oh, and don't forget to get her a brilliant Christmas present."

Kit pulled her coat on, eyes already on the door. "I got that a month ago. It's a bracelet she was admiring at a jeweller's. Almost cost a month's pay, but she's worth living off porridge for a while."

Shannon chuckled. "I doubt she'd let you live off porridge. Anyway, you hurry off and speak to your squeeze. I'll call you a little after midnight. If you're asleep, I'll try again tomorrow."

Kit wrapped her scarf around her neck. "Smashing. Bye!"

She hurried out while already calling Laura. No reply on the mobile. With freezing fingers, she dialled Howard Hall's landline number instead.

A warm, soft voice answered, "Laura Howard speaking."

Kit breathed out one heartfelt word, "Honey!"

Chapter Three

PINKY, WHERE ART THOU?

K it was asleep when the phone call came in. More interestingly, in Kit's opinion, was that she was asleep in the master bedroom at Howard Hall, naked and spooned in Laura's safe embrace when the phone rang.

Kit scrambled for her mobile on the bedside table as fast as she could. Laura hadn't had much time for sleeping lately, so any hours she could get tonight should be undisturbed.

Kit tapped the answer button, grabbed a blanket from the end of the bed, and snuck out of the bedroom before answering, "Hey, Shannon."

"Hey, Kit. Sorry it's so late."

Kit walked farther down the hallway so as not to be heard, shivering violently despite the blanket she was wrapped in.

Stupid freezing Edwardian manor house.

"Not a problem," she said. "So, can you talk about the 'personal' thing now?"

"Yes. I won't beat about the bush. It's something that's gone missing, and Rachel seems convinced I've lost it."

"Okay. So that's why she's cheesed off. What exactly is the thing?"

"Well, that's what makes it personal. And why I'm calling you now and not telling you in the pub."

Kit wiggled her toes to keep them warm despite the cold wooden floor. "I'm intrigued. Go on."

"It's… Pinky."

Kit's toes stilled, as confused as the rest of her. "It's what now?"

"Pinky."

She rolled her eyes. "Yes, Shannon, I heard what you said. I just don't know what a pinky is. As in a pinky finger? Or some sort of pink plush toy?"

Shannon groaned uncomfortably. "Toy is about right, but there's nothing plush about it. Look, this is very intimate. You can't tell anyone."

With a clue of where this was going, Kit closed her eyes. "Of course. All secrets are safe with me."

A few seconds passed in chafing silence.

Then Shannon sighed. "Pinky… is Rachel's favourite strap-on."

"Right."

"It vibrates."

Kit scratched an eyebrow. "Okay."

"And it's pink."

"Makes sense."

"And Rachel loves it because she says it's, well, the exact right size. Hits the right spots, you know?"

"Uh-huh," Kit said, aware that her voice had gone up in pitch.

Shannon seemed to have thought better of this conversation. "This is too much information for friends, right?

13

Especially ones who've only known each other for like half a year."

"No, no," Kit reassured her. "It's fine. I think we've both met those couples who tell you a hell of a lot more than this after only knowing you for a couple of hours. Especially after a few drinks. But we're a little too—"

"Sober," Shannon interrupted.

"I was going to say *English*. But sure, that, too. I suppose it's more accurate to say that we haven't had the sort of friendship where we talk a lot about our sex lives." Kit opened her eyes and squinted up at the high ceiling. "But maybe that should change. After all, Pinky sounds pretty awesome. Maybe I should've asked Laura to buy me one for Christmas," she joked.

"See, that's the thing. All the online shops I checked no longer stock this model. They have plenty of other ones, but Rachel likes this one because, as I said, it…"

"Fits perfectly," Kit supplied. "And you can't guarantee that these others will, even if they're the same size, because most strap-ons are different in their bends and shapes. I get the picture."

"Then you know what has to be done," Shannon said seriously.

"Original Pinky must be located."

"Exactly."

Kit blew out a breath. "Well, the first thing to ask is where Pinky could've gone. I assume you've scoured the house?"

"Top to bottom. At least once a day for the last five days."

"Okay, I hate to ask this, because we're again stepping into territory where we haven't ventured, but when was Pinky… last in action?"

"Five days ago. We used Pinky at night and then I cleaned it before going to work in the morning."

"Gotcha. And you don't have a cleaner?"

"No."

"Hm." Kit chewed the inside of her cheek. "Any visitors?"

"I figured you might ask that," Shannon said. "We've had Matt and Josh over for after-work drinks twice, Rajesh popped in while walking Phyllis three days ago, Steve Hallard and some woman he met online popped in for tea on Sunday, and yesterday Mabel Baxter came in to complain because our Christmas decorations were too merry."

Kit gulped as the image of Mabel popped into her head: a woman as wrinkly as a raisin with constantly pursed lips and a knitted hat pulled down halfway over her eyes year-round. "Blimey, I hope it wasn't Mabel who took it."

Shannon muttered, "Tell me about it."

"This woman Steve brought over. You don't know her?"

"Not at all. *He* barely knew her since it was a blind date. A failed one, I'd say. I think he was taking her for a stroll and popping into the houses they passed because the date was awful and he was bored."

Kit pulled the blanket tighter around her shivering body. "Okay, I'll find a way to chat to Steve about this woman without revealing what I'm looking for. It makes sense that she would've nicked Pinky, though. If the date was that bad, she might've needed it, if you know what I mean."

"Ugh, Kit! I don't want to think about anyone else using it. "

15

"Fine, fine. Sorry. Anyway, I'll start with chatting to Steve. Have you talked to Matt and Josh at all?"

"Yep, I tried to fish for any sign that they were having a laugh. You know, pranking us or something."

"And?" Kit asked, looking towards the bedroom door and hoping that her absence hadn't woken Laura.

"No joy. They seemed perfectly innocent for once. And, in all honestly, they're terrible at keeping secrets. Especially amusing ones. They'd start giggling or teasing me if they'd taken Pinky, I'm sure of it."

"So they're probably in the clear. Okay, keep an eye on them. I'm pretty sure Rajesh and Mabel aren't the stealing types. They wouldn't want Pinky or recognise what it was either." A thought popped into her head. "Oh, there's a point. Was it just the dildo or the whole harness?"

"Only the vibrating dildo. The harness is wash-proof, so it went into the washing machine and then safely back into the box."

"Right. Well, I'll—"

There was a creak. Kit squinted into the dark, wishing she'd put her glasses on. Was that a door opening at the other end of the hallway? There was a click of a light switch, and the sconces along the hallway came on.

Bollocks.

"What on earth?" Tom mumbled while shuffling closer.

"Shh! Your sister's sleeping and I'm on the phone!"

"Ah, Kit, it's you. Are you pretending to be a ghost? For a moment I thought you were my great-uncle Edmund. He's supposed to haunt Howard Hall, but he was humongous."

"Huh? What are you on about?" Kit looked down at

her body wrapped in a white blanket. "Oh, right. Yeah. Funny. It's a blanket, though. Ghosts use sheets."

"Fair point." He yawned. "So, my virtuous sister got a woman into bed again? She's getting more cherry pie than I am these days."

Kit's tired, distracted brain tried to focus. "What do you mean by cherry pi— Oh." She gave him a death glare. "Firstly, I'm the only one in her bed. Secondly, bugger off! I'm on the phone."

He scratched his armpit through his striped, preppy Jack Wills pyjamas. "Calm down, I only got up to get some water. Enjoy your phone call. I'll see you over breakfast, unless you get thrown out because Little Miss Perfect is *busy*," he sneered.

Kit was about to give him a piece of her mind. After all, most of Laura's busyness was due to the work for their family firm, securing *his* pension fund and keeping him in pricy pyjamas, while Tom did nothing more than the occasional networking event. But he wandered off, and Kit was suddenly aware of having left Shannon waiting.

"Shannon? You still there?"

"Yep."

"Sorry, that was Tom. To be honest, I didn't know he was here. He's usually out until early morning. Anyway, he didn't hear anything. Where were we?"

"We decided I'm going to keep an eye on Josh and Matt and see if they giggle about stealing Pinky. You're going to chat to Steve about his date, without giving away why you're talking to him."

"Great. I'll get back to you when I've quizzed Steve."

"All right, I'll ring or text if there's any more info."

They said their goodnights, and Kit padded back to the bedroom. She replaced the blanket and the phone before gingerly getting back under the duvet. She closed her eyes and searched for sleep. It was hard with her mind eager to dig further into the mystery of Pinky. Who takes someone else's sex toy? And why?

Laura's arm snaked around her waist and pulled her back into spooning. Kit gave a happy sigh, snuggled in, and slowed her breathing. Sleep was on the cards again.

Chapter Four

EIGHT DAYS 'TIL CHRISTMAS

K it rushed along the high street on Greengage Square. She was on her afternoon break but had decided to spend it in search of Pinky instead of having tea in the library's tiny excuse for a kitchen.

She shivered and thrust her hands into the pockets of her winter coat. Considering it was now the seventeenth of December, it would have been nice if there'd been a dusting of snow. Instead it was windy, and the pavements were slick with rain that had fallen that morning. Still, the weather hadn't slowed down the Christmas market, which was now in full whack. The little wooden huts had all been filled by Greengage locals, selling everything from home-made cakes to knitted scarves to pottery of varying quality.

Kit side-eyed the huts. She'd hoped that the start of the Christmas market would mean that her girlfriend had more time for her. Instead, Laura was now busy trying to manage the issues that the market had brought up. This included Greengagers fighting over who got the best hut, how to fund the extra electricity bill, how loud the Christmas music was allowed to be played, and if "Santa

Baby" was an appropriate song despite the possible euphemism of the line "come and trim my Christmas tree".

Kit had asked if there was anything she could do to help. Laura had groaned and suggested that she keep well away from the events committee, adding, "Please be patient and know that I miss you."

Kit looked away from the Christmas market. She wasn't wasting her tea break on that. She was heading to Steve Hallard's newsagent… or off-licence… whatever he called his little shop on the other side of the square. She had popped in the night after the phone call with Shannon to interview Steve about his date, only to be told by the teenager behind the counter that Steve was visiting relatives on the mainland. Even more annoyingly, he wouldn't return until the seventeenth.

Now, here she was, on her way to speak to the man who had once given her a warning about hurting Greengage's favourite daughter. That she could forgive. It was nice that the islanders were as fond of, and loyal to, Laura as she was to them. What was harder to swallow was that he'd done it on the night when Kit and Laura were about to be intimate for the first time.

Although it wasn't his fault. That whole night was a disaster. Funny in hindsight, but still a disaster.

With a look at her watch, Kit speed-walked the last bit of the way and stepped inside. She peered past all the magazines, sweets, and random bits of stationery to the counter. Yes, Steve was back and busy at work.

She waited until he had finished serving his customer, then sauntered over while taking her thick scarf off.

"Hey there, Steve. You all right, mate?"

"Hello, Kit." He did a double take. "Huh, weird to see

you out of your uniform. You know, the biker jacket and those tatty, green trainers."

Kit fought to keep an offended look off her features.

It's a fitted leather jacket. And the Converse are blue and a little faded, not tatty.

Unaware of her thoughts, Steve chuckled at his own comment before adding, "I'm doing well, thanks. You?"

She cleared her throat. "Doing all right. Well, except that I'm struggling to get into the holiday cheer."

"Ah, that's a shame."

"I suppose. Anyway, I'm trying not to whinge about it. After all, it'll be Christmas no matter how I feel about it."

"True enough. So, is there anything I can get you?"

Kit undid her coat, trying not to roast in the warm shop. "No, not really. I popped in to see how you were. Did you have a good week with your family?"

"I did. I had to see them now as they bugger off to Mallorca over Christmas." He examined her. "It's nice of you to take such an interest in what I'm doing. Unusual, but nice."

Kit tried to look casual. "I suppose with Laura being so busy with the events committee stuff regarding the Christmas market and all the Gage Farm business, I need people to chat to. Speaking of which… I was talking to Shannon a few days ago."

His features softened. "Ah, Shannon's a love, isn't she?"

"She is." Kit glanced around as if checking that no one was listening. "You know, she mentioned that you had a hot date a while back?"

He scratched his balding head. "I had a date. I don't know about 'hot', though."

"Not Miss Right, huh?"

"She was lovely but not my type. My cousin up in

21

London works with her and thought that we'd be a good match because we're both what he calls 'wholesome'. However, in her case, wholesome means she likes to keep her interactions platypus. No, that's not it. Plap… Plat..."

"Platonic?" Kit suggested.

He clicked his fingers. "That's the one."

"What's wrong with that?"

"Nothing. But she strongly disliked romance, sex, and such. When I talked about finding a lover to settle down with, she said that no one used their brains anymore, it was all about swollen crotches and soppy hearts. She hadn't even wanted to go on a date, she only agreed because she owed my cousin a favour."

Seems like she'd neither know what Pinky was or have an interest in stealing it, Kit thought. *Unless she took it on principle, to make sure no one else has sex?*

"Ah, I'm sorry to hear that," she said. "Sounds like she was pretty preachy about it. Was she mean to you because you like sex?"

He gave her a questioning glance but answered. "No, she didn't seem to mind people who had amorous encounters. She simply pitied them and tried to avoid them, I'd say."

Kit fussed with her scarf, wondering if she should've put in more small talk before the interrogation. "Shannon mentioned that you and your date swung by their place. Were you looking for sympathy? Or merely hoping they'd offer you a stiff drink to get you through the date?"

The joke seemed to relax him again. He chuckled before saying, "We went there to see Rach. She's great at breaking the ice and providing normal chitchat. I often seek her out to pitch in when my own social skills let me down. Anything else you wanted to know about my love life, nosey Londoner?"

Kit laughed. "As I said, I'm clearly getting lonely and bothering anyone who'll chat to me. You'll be safe now, though. I have to get back to work. We'll have to catch up more soon. I'm sorry that your date didn't work out."

"It's all right. You know, I actually think she and I could've been good friends or a nonphysical couple if it hadn't been for the fact that she loves tweed. I can't stand tweed. Never could. Can you imagine being with someone who wears a tweed jacket with tweed trousers and has a tweedy scarf over her hair? Who does that?"

Kit searched for an answer. "Um. She did, I suppose? Well, I guess it was sign that it wasn't meant to be if you couldn't overlook the fabric of her clothes."

He squinted at her.

Great. You pissed him off.

When would she learn that logic and common sense didn't work with the people of Greengage? They had their hang-ups, their superstitions, and foibles by the bucket loads. Questioning these things never got her anywhere.

"That's none of my business, though," she said with what she hoped was a winning smile. "I should get going. Thanks again for the chat."

Steve got distracted by another customer coming in, one he looked happier to see. "That's all right, Kit," he said absently. "Keep an eye on our Laura for us and try to enjoy Christmas. After all, you only get one per year, and there's only eight days left 'til the big day!"

The customer squealed with delight, and Kit took her chance to sneak out before they could break out in Christmas carols.

Once outside, Kit stopped to button her coat and put

her scarf back on. The Christmas market was brimming with people despite the workweek not being over.

Oh, Greengage, you're showing your age with all these pensioners.

She headed back to the library. When she passed a group of people by a hut selling rocks painted as Mr and Mrs Santa Claus, she heard a man say, "Why the market didn't open earlier, I'll never know. Who blooming well wants a Christmas market that starts in the middle of December? It'll only be open for a few days."

The woman next to him nodded. "Aye, it shows what happens when you trust the events committee to arrange these things. The council should've been in charge of it. It's that snooty Laura Howard and her posh friends, spending all their time chatting about cricket and where to store your gold bars."

True to her London upbringing, Kit was about to scoff and storm off. But this was Greengage. Here, if you had the answer, you supplied it. Otherwise, strange rumours brewed. If Kit didn't put a stop to this now, soon everyone'd be saying that the events committee was busy dipping their privates in gold and playing cricket with them.

With that in mind, Kit took a deep breath and said, "Sorry to interfere, but I've got to correct you. It's this late due to the huts only becoming available a short while ago. And that was when the committee's Mabel Baxter and Ethel Rosenthal, both penniless pensioners I hasten to add, came up with the idea of having the market."

They stared at Kit as if she was some exotic animal who had wandered into their midst, so she carried on. "If it's a success, it'll be planned better and further in advance next year. So, get to buying some Santa rocks here, try to be nice to the few tourists we've gathered, and you can have the market on the first of December next year." She began to walk off but stopped, turned, and added, "Oh, and Laura Howard is the only reason that the Christmas market happened at all. The council didn't care, and the others on the events committee couldn't arrange a piss-up in a brewery. She's giving up time she doesn't have to try to make this work out. I'd suggest showing her some respect."

A few heartbeats of silence ensued.

She went to leave again, but the man who had first spoken beckoned to her. "Good afternoon, Kit. It is Kit, isn't it? I'm a proud library user, so I know who you are. Actually, I think everyone on the island does." He looked to the others, who all nodded. "You made quite the splash when you became involved with Laura. I guess that's why you know as much about this as you do. And you have a point, of course. We're simply whinging, as you do in good company on a cold winter's day. Nothing personal, everyone loves little Laura Howard."

"Mm. Then maybe you give her a break? She's posh but not rich, and she certainly doesn't sit around chatting." Kit smiled to take the sting out of her words and added, "Enjoy the market, and, as I say, try to buy as much as you can to support it. I hope to see you at the library."

She headed back to work with more of a sense of the sort of people her girlfriend had to deal with on a daily basis. It amplified the lovesick longing in Kit's heart. She picked up her phone to call Laura, ready to press her on if she was celebrating Christmas at Howard Hall with her brother or walking over to Kit's cottage to spend the day with her.

With a groan, though, she reminded herself of how stressed Laura was and how little she could control or predict her schedule. More importantly, Kit remembered what she'd just told those complainers back there.

Give Laura a break.

Kit put the phone away. She could wait until Laura had the time and energy to call her.

Chapter Five

PINKY OF THE BELLS

After dinner that night, Kit phoned Shannon. As she waited for a reply, she scratched Phyllis behind one of her unevenly sized ears. Rajesh was on a date, and Kit, still lonely, had offered to babysit the lazy dog even though Phyllis was fine on her own.

Phyllis lifted her head and leaned into the scratching, which was the first time Kit had seen her move all night. After a few rings, Shannon finally picked up.

"Hiya, Kit. What's up?"

"Hey. Not much. Is this a bad time?"

"No, the pub's quiet. Apparently, most of our regulars are out bell-ringing."

"Really? Well, it's Greengage, so I suppose bell-ringing is actually one of the more normal things happening around here." Kit kept scratching behind Phyllis' ear. Maybe if she kept the mutt awake, Kit could get her to come along for her evening walk. "Anyway, I wanted to let you know that I've spoken to Steve. It seems his date was the asexual, aromantic, cerebral type who only wanted to get off the island fast. I very much doubt that she would've stolen Pinky."

"Ah, bollocks. Oh well, it was worth a try."

"Agreed. If we can't find the culprit we might have to revisit, but as I say, she seems an unlikely candidate."

"Mm. So, what's the next move?"

Kit noticed a sound like a small tractor and realised it was Phyllis snoring. She stopped scratching the sleeping dog's ear. "I suppose the next thing to do is talk to Rajesh."

"Sure. I have to say, though, I can't think why he would take Pinky. Unless he meant to use it as a hand blender for when he makes those weirdly bitter curries?"

Kit laughed. "I doubt it, but I'll ask. Unless it turns out to be Rajesh, I should probably talk to Matt and Josh next. I know you've spoken to them, but they might be more likely to confess if I'm asking."

"True. Lately, though, they've been droning on and on about trying to be more mature. So, as I said before, I really don't think they had anything to do with this."

"Okay, well, it doesn't hurt to keep asking. Pinky has to be somewhere."

"You're right. Thanks for carrying on with the search. Rachel's still in a dreadful mood, and her tetchiness seems to be switching to sadness, which is even harder for me to deal with. Breaks my heart when she's not happy."

"I know what you mean. Earlier today someone whinged about how Laura arranged the Christmas market. Not only did it make me defensive, it also made me think of how much time she's spent on this and for how little reward. I wish I could fix that."

Shannon hummed. "Well, as I'm sure you know, Laura doesn't do these things because she wants a reward. She simply wants to do something nice for the people around her. Helping others makes her happy."

Kit smiled so wide it made her cheeks ache. "True. Anyway, I'll swing by tomorrow night and talk to the guys. That sound okay?"

"Sure, pop in anytime you want. We're here every night except Sundays."

"Okay, great. Bye," Kit said and hung up.

She quickly tapped out a text to Laura:

Hey baby, I hope you're okay. I love you and I'm so proud of all the work you do. Don't stress about getting back to me. I know you love me and miss me. Almost as much as I miss you. (Kidding!)

She poked Phyllis in the fattest part of her belly and said, "Right, you! Since I hate going for a run and it's too cold for you to play in the park, we're gonna take a long walk."

Phyllis made a groaning sound, making Kit chuckle. "None of that, lazy. Let's go get your favourite squeaky toy, and then it's walkies."

🐾

Next morning at the library, Kit stole a quiet moment to chat with her ex-landlord.

"Rajesh, can I ask you something?"

He stopped humming "Carol of the Bells" and knitted his bushy eyebrows. "Even if I say no, you'll ask." He shook his head at her. "At least now I only have to put up with it at work. I hated when you'd start asking me questions at the flat, when we'd barely woken up."

Kit rolled her eyes. "It's not my fault you're comatose at the breakfast table. Anyway, it's only a quick question."

"Fine," he said as he scanned a returned book back into the system. "Ask, but I'm going to keep working."

"Sure. So, um, when you last visited Rach and Shannon, did you happen to pick up something that you might have found lying around?"

"What are you on about, Katherine?"

Kit fidgeted with her glasses. "Um, well, Shannon said that they had lost something. I think she said it was something… pink?"

"Pink? No, I certainly didn't pick up anything pink. There's nothing to pick up at their house anyway. They keep that place unnaturally clean and never have clutter," he said without looking up from the book he was cleaning jam off of. At least, Kit hoped that was jam. After a moment, he frowned. "What kind of pink things could you lose?"

Kit shrugged. "Anything, I suppose. A hairbrush, a bottle of lotion, a book. A lot of things can be pink."

"Mm, I suppose you're right," he said and went back to the jam-wiping.

Kit observed Rajesh for a while, trying to think of reasons he might have for stealing Pinky and then lying about it. He did have a prankster trait, but it usually only came out when he was talking to her. It also never lasted long since he couldn't keep a straight face. He certainly wasn't the type to lie if he'd been caught in the act. No, it was unlikely that Rajesh was the strap-on thief. Of course, Kit had never really suspected him. It was more likely to be one of the guys running Pub 42.

At that moment, a young mother and her toddler came up to the counter. The toddler opened its toothless mouth wide, ready to nibble on a copy of *To the Lighthouse* that was nestled in the mother's arms. Kit pushed the mystery of Pinky aside and hurried over to serve them. And rescue the book.

❧

At lunch, Kit checked her phone and saw a missed call from Laura. With a little yelp of joy, she called back, only to find that the line was occupied. She went to unpack her sandwich and make tea, then tried calling again. Laura was still on another call. Kit sat down and began eating. Her sandwich was filled with turkey and stuffing, in a vain attempt to force the Christmas spirit into her stomach, if not into her mind. It sort of worked, at least as far as the sandwiches being more celebratory with this filling than her usual unsweetened peanut butter.

She tried Laura's phone one last time, but it was still occupied. She sighed and dialled Aimee instead. Her best friend picked up right away.

"Hey, Aimee."

"Hello, lesbian."

"You twit, what have I told you about greeting me by my sexuality?"

"That it's silly?"

"Exactly. Anyway, how are you and, more importantly, how is my godson?"

"George is good. He's advanced from playing with his wooden blocks all the time to also building with Duplo. His towers are getting higher and higher. And they trip me up more and more. So, yeah, he's happy."

"What about you?"

Aimee made an, for her, unusually simpering noise. "Blissfully happy. I think Carl might be the man of my dreams, and if you say that's sappy, I'll kill you. Twice."

Kit swallowed some tea. "Okay. Well, I'm glad you're happy, mate. Is he celebrating Christmas at your place?"

"Nope, we're going to his parents in Winchester. It'll be the first time I meet them."

"Ooh, sounds like things are getting serious if you're meeting his parents."

"His whole family, actually. Or at least nineteen of them. It's a bit scary but most of all it makes me feel guilty because I haven't let Carl meet my parents yet. You know how judgemental they can be. I don't think they'll like him. He's got very little ambition, he can seem uncaring sometimes, and, well, he's not Korean."

"Ah, right. Well, as long as you and George like him, who cares what they think? They disapprove of everything you like and everything you do since your divorce."

"Yeah, I miss the golden days of being accepted and appreciated. Now the only thing they seem to like about my life is that I'm still in touch with you."

"Weird!"

"No, not really," Aimee said quietly. "You've got a job you excel at, an excellent partner, and you're independent. That's all they ever wanted for me."

"I don't feel so independent right now. I feel lonely. I don't live with you anymore. Or Rajesh. Laura is busy as the time. I don't really socialise with anyone. And bloody Christmas is coming up. If this is being independent, it sucks."

"Sorry, sweetheart."

Kit pinched the back of her hand when she realised

she'd made something that was about Aimee revolve around herself. "What I wanted to say, Aimee, was that while I'm glad to be something your parents approve of, I'm sorry that it's not one of the things that you have achieved. Like your job, your nice apartment. Or, you know, that perfect toddler who builds trip hazards."

Aimee hummed. "But then you did help me get this part-time job and apartment in one of your many 'Kit can fix it' projects. Granted, you had nothing to do with the making of George."

Kit scrunched up her nose so much she worried her glasses might fall down it. "I sure as hell didn't. Yuck."

"Oi! I've said it a million times, what's the point in having a lesbian best friend unless she fancies me? At least enough not to be grossed out by the idea of making a George with me."

"Look, I know you're only messing with me, but I recently ate so I think we should stop this borderline-incestuous conversation. Go back to talking about your parents or switch to my problematic love life instead," Kit whinged.

"Your love life? Problematic? You found the perfect partner! Laura's kind, cute, and rich."

Kit spun her mug, watching the tea slosh around. "Laura wouldn't agree with rich. Fruit farms don't exactly rake it in, and her family fortune dwindled generations ago when Howard Hall started needing pots of money for renovations. What little is left Tom seems to be frittering away."

"Kit, I know that. I lived there for a short while, remember? Laura can still afford a cleaner and a cook to come in every afternoon. In my book, she's rich."

"Fair point."

"Anyway, Laura's all those great things, and then, for some reason she fell in love with *you*," Aimee teased. "I mean, it's bizarre, but not problematic."

"The fact that I can't get more than two hours alone with her at a time is."

"Yeah, you mentioned that she's still busy."

"Mm. I've been trying to leave her alone, to not stress her or seem too clingy. But I miss her."

"Well," Aimee said in a maternal tone, "if she's so busy and stressed, don't you think she'd appreciate her girlfriend coming over with something nice to eat, a sympathetic ear, and offering a neck massage or something?"

Kit tapped her fingers against the mug. "Huh. You may have a point." She gazed into the tea. "Why didn't I think of that?"

"Because you're a plant pot," Aimee replied.

Kit rolled her eyes. "I think I prefer it when you straight-up call me silly to when you start using imagery in your insults."

"I prefer the poetic approach, mate. As a bookworm, I thought you'd appreciate that. Now go shelve a book or something."

"God, you're a nuisance," Kit said with a laugh. "Say hello to the little builder from me. I love you."

"I love you, too, plant pot. Bye."

Kit pushed the phone into the tiny pocket of her skinny jeans and sat back. As she finished her tea, she pondered what to bring over to Howard Hall when she surprised Laura.

Chapter Six

LET'S TALK ABOUT SEX. AND CHRISTMAS

The workday was finally at an end, and Kit was finally at Laura's door, waiting for her to answer the ring of Howard Hall's antiquated doorbell.

The door flew open, and Laura grabbed Kit by the lapels of her coat to pull her into a kiss. Then into a hug. Then through the door and into Howard Hall.

The warmth of the house gave Kit almost as much pleasure as the hugs and kisses. December was making itself known now, shouting from the rooftops that winter had dug its heels in.

"You knew it was me then?" Kit teased. "Or do you greet everyone like this?"

Laura blushed. "Of course not. I happened to be by the window while on a call to a supplier and saw you arriving." She took Kit's scarf and coat and hung them up for her. Then she pointed to the paper bag in Kit's hand and asked, "Oh! What's that?"

"Fish and chips. I also brought two bottles of that new tonic you like. I assumed you had gin knocking about somewhere."

Laura leaned in for a kiss and sneakily peered into the bag as she did so. "You know me so well, dearest. And thank you for bringing food, I'm positively starving."

She headed for the stairs leading to the huge, Victorian-styled basement kitchen. Kit followed her, asking, "Haven't eaten much today?"

Laura smoothed down her auburn curls, which had begun to frizz. "No. During lunch I had to be on the phone to a supplier. At the same time as I read a complaint from one of the sellers at the Christmas market. It's been manic."

"But you ate *something*, right?"

"I managed to scoff a bag of crisps and a bottle of juice. That was all, and, as you know, I am not one for skipping meals."

"No, not to mention the snacks you usually have. No wonder you're hungry."

They arrived down in the kitchen, which always seemed abandoned when Howard Hall's part-time cook wasn't there making soups and preserves, or whatever she did every afternoon. There were sprigs of holly above the huge, old stove, but other than that, there were no Christmas ornaments anywhere.

Kit watched as Laura took out some plates, noticing that her girlfriend was paler than usual. There were bags under her eyes as well.

Kit grabbed the cutlery that Laura was holding and put them down on the countertop. She caressed a few curls out of Laura's face while murmuring, "You're working too hard, babe."

Laura looked down. "I know. I also know it means I've been neglecting you. Work is work and that always keeps me busy, but…" She closed her eyes for a moment. "I thought things would slow down after the market was up and running. Clearly I was naïve. If the events committee decide they want to arrange another Christmas market next year, I'm bowing out. I'm so sorry that I haven't had much time for you."

"Hey, it's okay, honey. When I started dating you, I knew you were devoted to Greengage and the people on it and that you always put others before yourself. I knew what I was getting into." Kit sighed. "And while I have been whinging about you not having time for me, I'm more worried about the fact that you don't have time for yourself." She put two fingers under Laura's chin and lifted her face until they were eye to eye again. "Are you getting enough sleep?"

Laura kissed Kit's fingers and then took her hand. "Not really. I feel guilty because I'm not spending enough time at work, not enough time sorting out the market, and certainly not enough time with you. That all makes it hard to sleep. Also, I can't shut my thoughts off at night." She edged closer to Kit with a tentative smile. "It doesn't help that since I work well into the evenings, I so rarely have my favourite teddy bear with me in bed. Will you spend the night here tonight?"

"The only thing that could stop this teddy bear from staying would be you telling me to go."

"Well." Laura paused to smirk. Kit was glad to see a little of her usual energy in her eyes. "That's certainly not going to happen."

Kit squeezed her hand. "Great! First, let's get some food in you. I'll plate up the fish and chips if you go to whichever fancy drink trolley is nearest and grab a bottle of gin."

Laura closed her eyes and gave a satisfied sigh. "Ah, the

relief of not being the one giving the orders."

"Hey, if you want someone to order you around tonight, that can be achieved," Kit purred. "Hell, if you'd like, I can even tie you to the bed to keep you from feeling that you have to be at the wheel."

Laura winked. "As long as I'm not too tired, that sounds like a plan." She took out two highball glasses. "Now I'm going upstairs to find some gin. There's lemon slices in the fridge and ice in the freezer, obviously. See you up in the dining room."

She walked up the stairs. Kit couldn't stop herself from watching her go.

When she was gone, Kit realised that her knees had gone weak at the sight of Laura's perfectly fitted, imposing Savile Row suit.

And that her heart had gone weak at the glimpse of what looked like black socks with red apples on them that Laura had paired it with.

The two sides of my brilliant fruit farmer; all refined business until you get the top layer off. Then it's all cuteness.

Kit dished up the food and prepared to give it a quick blast in the microwave.

Let's get her fed, drunk, and see if she wants to get laid or only cuddled tonight.

As the microwave whirred, Kit realised she was happy. No matter what they were going to do, she had a whole evening with Laura. Maybe they'd even talk about Christmas. Or she could finally tell Laura about *Operation: Find Pinky.*

Dinner and two gin and tonics into the evening, Kit had

ramped up the flirting since Laura didn't seem too tired to be amorous.

Now, Kit leaned in for a kiss before crooning, "As I said, I'll call the shots and do all the work. I know you're not used to that, but it's never too late to learn something new. All you have to do is lie there and tell me what feels good. Sound okay?"

"Sounds heavenly," Laura breathed. "I do, however, think I'll need some sort of dessert first to give me energy to, um, finish."

"Good idea. Knowing you, there'll be some biscuits somewhere, right?"

Laura smiled. "Obviously! There's ice cream and some leftover jam sponge, too."

"Smashing. Then we can get a sweet treat and maybe talk about Christmas? I haven't brought it up because you've been busy, and I assumed you'd have to spend Christmas here with your shitty brother. Family duty and all that gubbins. But I'm hoping to see some of you and hand over your present at least."

Laura reached over the table and took Kit's hand. "My dearest, beautiful darling. Of course—"

She got no further as the house phone picked that moment to ring. Laura let go of Kit's hand and rubbed her forehead. "You're going to kill me, but I have to take that. I was sort of expecting a call from a colleague regarding a possible marketing alliance. He could only ring tonight if it's to be discussed before Christmas, but, to be honest, I was hoping he'd forget."

Kit picked up a napkin and wiped her mouth. "It's okay! Go ahead and take it. I'm not going anywhere."

Laura rushed off to the phone, and Kit stifled a sigh. She sipped her third G&T and waited. Minutes passed.

Kit looked around the threadbare but sophisticated room with that same feeling of being out of place that Howard Hall usually gave her. She was used to grubby little London flats.

I bet it'd look less intimidating with some Christmas decorations.

Another few minutes oozed by. Then Kit put her glass down.

I might as well be productive.

She fished out her phone and texted Shannon that Rajesh didn't seem a likely culprit and that the next move would indeed be for her to chat to Matt and Josh.

It only took a moment for Shannon to text back that that all sounded fine and to thank her again for helping out.

Kit finished her drink and put her phone on the table. She waited for the woman she loved and was surprised to find herself humming "Jingle Bells" under her breath. She refilled her own glass and Laura's, making sure that Laura had a little extra gin to make up for the drink she'd missed.

Just as Kit finished her cocktail making, Laura came back. Her usually sweet face was set in a determined look. She placed her phone on the table, right on top of Kit's. Then she took Kit's hand and said, "That's it! Enough of the chatter and distractions. Right now, I want to make love with the woman I adore. Then I want to sleep in her arms. Sound agreeable?"

"Abso-bloody-lutely!" Kit shouted and jumped up from her seat.

They hurried upstairs to the master bedroom, all discussions of Christmas or explanations about the Pinky search out the window.

Chapter Seven

I'LL BE HOME FOR CHRISTMAS... WHAT ABOUT YOU?

W hite, wintry light was prodding at Kit's closed eyelids.

Buggering bollocks. It can't be morning. We only fell asleep a minute ago.

When spending the night at Howard Hall, Kit usually woke up to Laura getting ready for work. She was always needed out in the orchards or down in the office long before Kit had to open up the library.

This morning, when Kit finally agreed to open her eyes, it was clear that Laura wasn't just getting ready for work. She was doing the elaborate dance of someone trying to hurry but still be quiet. Also, her lips were moving in what looked like a tirade of the f-word. Considering Laura's harshest curse word was usually "blooming", this was worrying.

"Everything all right?' Kit asked.

Laura startled before melting into a smile. "Oh, good morning, dearest. Honestly? Nothing's all right. I made the mistake of checking my emails a moment ago and saw that there was a complaint regarding copyright infringement of a logo."

"What?"

"Yes. Obviously, it came from South Gage Farm, like most far-fetched, time-wasting nonsense does. How dare they? As if *they* haven't copied everything that Gage Farm has done ever since my parents ran it."

Kit raised herself up to lean on her elbows. "Yeah, I remember when you and I were about to start dating and you guys were creating that logo. That was April. South Gage Farm changed theirs last week, right? So where the hell do they get off saying that you have copied them?"

Laura shook her head. "There's no rhyme or reason to their complaints. They merely like to cause trouble and to whinge. Anyway, I have to deal with it because it looks bad to the public."

Kit rubbed sleep out of her eyes. "Yeah, of course. You get going. I'll wash up and get dressed. Then I'll scrounge up some breakfast and bring something to you out in the office before I head off to the library."

Laura paused while buttoning her shirt. "Really? That would be wonderful. I can get tea and coffee down in the office, but the only food I have there is a pack of raisins, and, quite frankly, I'm going to need more than that in me to deal with the Stevensons."

"Good god, yes," Kit muttered.

The Stevensons ran the competing fruit farm on the island and were notoriously stubborn and rude. And due to an ancient feud and infected dispute over Gage Farm, they were eager to cause any Howard some trouble. Especially ever since their golden son and heir had run off with Laura's aunt.

Kit stayed there, warm and sleepy, and watched Laura

do her hair and makeup. There was something so intimate and fascinating about watching all the little rituals that went into making the sweet, soft, freckled woman she had cuddled all night into the polished businesswoman who was now putting on her suit jacket.

"You know, I can't take my eyes off you," Kit whispered.

Laura turned to face her, bashfully biting her lip. "You say the sweetest things. I wish I didn't have to leave. More accurately, I wish I could take you with me everywhere. Does that sound clingy? Or weird?"

Kit smiled. "I'm usually the one asking you that. But no, it sounds great, actually."

Laura rescued her phone from the bottle of perfume that had fallen on it, then walked over and sat down on the bed next to Kit. "Maybe when things quiet down at Gage Farm and this infernal Christmas market is over, we can take a holiday somewhere? Just you and me. I don't care where we go, as long as I can be with you and not have all these interruptions."

Kit reached out and adjusted the lapel on Laura's suit jacket. "I'd like that. Or maybe we should simply hide all the phones and stay in this bed for a month?"

Laura smiled and leaned down for a kiss. When their lips parted again, Laura's mobile rang.

"Speaking of phones," Kit quipped.

Laura glared at her mobile as if it had slapped her with a wet mop. Her knuckles were white where she gripped it.

"Um, baby?" Kit ventured. "You do know you can just turn it off, right?"

"Honestly? I think they'd still find a way to ring me. In fact, I think they'd find a way to ring me even if I was dead and buried in the mausoleum. And that place never has any reception."

Kit chuckled at Laura's despairing joke. "Anyway, you better answer that before we wake your daft brother and he comes stumbling in here."

"Yes, I'll answer it while I head down to the office. Thank you for bringing me food. Both last night and now for breakfast. You're an angel."

She didn't wait for a reply but hurried out while answering the call. Kit heard her say, "What is it now, Kipp?" as she barrelled down the stairs.

It was only when Kit lay back down on the plush pillows that she realised they still hadn't discussed what they were doing for Christmas.

That lunch hour, Kit walked into Pub 42. She saw Rachel behind the bar and Shannon waiting tables, and gave them both a wave before popping into the kitchen, the domain of the pub's male owners.

Next to a bowl of dark red cherries, Josh and Matt were arguing over which fruit worked best with duck, cherry or orange.

Weird. Why are they talking about that when the most complicated thing they serve here is quesadillas?

"Hey there," Kit greeted them. "Thinking about adding duck to the menu?"

Josh waved enthusiastically at her while Matt merely laughed and said, "Don't be daft. No one comes in here for anything more than usual pub grub. No, we were discussing what we're eating for Christmas since both our families have decided that they're not big fans of turkey."

Trying to hide her envy at the thought of a big family Christmas, Kit leaned casually against a wall. "Right, yeah, that makes sense. I'm sure it'll be lovely whatever you choose to eat. Anyway, I didn't come here to talk about Christmas. Or about food."

Josh tilted his head and raised his meticulous blond eyebrows. "Then what did you come here to talk about, love? You doing all right?"

"Yeah, I'm fine." Kit adjusted her glasses, realising that she'd now blown any chance of normal small talk leading into quizzing them about Pinky. What was up with her lately? It wasn't like her to be this frazzled over something like Christmas being a bit rubbish or missing a girlfriend. Sure, she was bad at being alone, but this was getting ridiculous.

"Hm, right, I'll come right out and ask this. Did you by chance play a prank on Rach and Shannon lately? It'll be our secret if you did."

They both stared at her as if she had sprouted big blue mushrooms on her head.

"A prank? What do you mean?" Matt asked.

"I mean…" Kit blew out a breath. "If you had joked around with Rach and Shannon. You know, maybe nicked something from them or hidden one of their things?"

Kit was met with confused blinking from both men, so she elaborated. "You're bound to have noticed that Shannon and Rach have been out of sorts over the last couple of weeks. Apparently that's because someone is messing about with them," Kit improvised.

The guys looked at each other. Matt shrugged, making Josh turn back to Kit to say, "Neither of us knows anything about that. Sure, we have a bantery type of friendship and we've played a few practical jokes on them before, but we're trying to cut down on that sort of behaviour."

Kit straightened up. "Now that you mention it, Shannon did say that the two of you are trying to be more grown-up."

They glanced at each other again and then Matt said, "You might as well tell her. Kit won't gossip."

Josh lit up, and soon Matt matched his smile.

Kit looked back and forth between the two lovebirds. "What's going on here?"

Josh squealed. "I'm so excited to tell someone! We've decided that after New Year's we're going to start the process to adopt. We've always wanted to be parents but haven't felt mature enough to take on the responsibility. Now, we've decided that we finally are."

"Or at least getting there," Matt corrected. "Which means we're not in the pranking business anymore."

Josh glanced towards the closed door before whispering, "However, I *have* noticed that something is going on with Rach and Shannon. To be honest, I just put it down to the usual manic stress around the holiday season."

Matt nodded and moved closer to Kit. "Same here. I'm sad to hear it's something more serious. If there's anything we can do to help, let us know."

Kit reached up and patted his beefy shoulder. "I'm sure if it doesn't work itself out, they'll come to you for help themselves. I know they think the world of you. Anyway, I better get going. Good luck with the duck," she paused to give them a cheeky grin, "and whatever it is you're meant to be cooking for *work*, lazy gits."

Laughing, Josh threw a pair of cherries at Kit and said, "Oh, bugger off! And good luck with figuring out what's bothering Rach and Shannon."

Kit caught the cherries and said, "No need for luck. It's all skill, mate. See you again soon!" She popped both cherries into her mouth, tossed their stems at the still-laughing Josh, and headed for the door.

As she came back out into the serving area and nodded a farewell to the busy Shannon, Kit mentally crossed Matt and Josh off the list of suspects. Shannon had been right; it wasn't them.

Kit braved the cold again, urgently searching her coat pockets for her gloves. While she spit the cherry pits into a bin, her brain whirred.

If it wasn't Matt and Josh who'd taken Pinky, and not Rajesh either, then she was back to Steve's date, right? Or could it have been someone else? Some visitor that Shannon had forgotten? Someone Rachel had invited when Shannon wasn't there? Maybe even a burglar? No, they would've noticed if they'd have a break-in. Surely no criminal broke in to only steal a vibrating, pink dildo.

Not without locating the harness to get the whole set at least.

She sniggered to herself at the thought.

Maybe Shannon and Rach haven't looked everywhere? Perhaps it'll roll out from underneath the sofa one day? So many questions, and here's me without a single answer.

Kit walked back toward the library with heavy steps.

Still no Pinky. Still not enough time with Laura. Still no holiday cheer.

A shop she passed was blaring out some Christmas song by Elvis, as if to taunt her. It was even more annoying that she couldn't remember the name of the song.

She straightened her back and stepped along with more vigour. She had told herself she wouldn't whinge anymore, and she was going to stick to that. She shook her head. It was ridiculous that she still didn't know if she was celebrating Christmas with her girlfriend, though. And even more ridiculous that she was afraid to ask. What was the worst thing that could happen? That she'd say no? That wasn't the end of the world.

Kit pulled her phone from her coat pocket and texted Laura a quick proclamation of love and a clear question of if they would spend Christmas together. Then she pushed the phone deep in her pocket and hurried back to work. When she got to the library door, her mobile vibrated with a reply from Laura.

Hey dearest
Please don't be too angry or disappointed, but the way things are going, especially now with this dispute over the logo, it looks like I'll be tied up for the foreseeable future. I've had to neglect so much paperwork and it's all mounting up. If I get time for a proper Christmas at home I would certainly like to spend it with you! But there is a risk that we'll have to do what we're doing now, steal what moments we can and hope that I can make it up to you after New Year's. I have to go, we'll talk more about this later. I love you so very much and I'm awfully sorry for being so rubbish.
xoxo

Kit kicked a pebble. At least now she knew. But what did she know? Not more than that Laura would probably be working over the holidays and that any Christmas celebration would be patchy.

It was a step forward because she knew that Laura

wanted to spend the holidays with her, but a step back because it was clear that any Christmas celebration they'd have would need to be improvised. Maybe some presents and a last-minute turkey sandwich? There'd be no Christmas decorating with Laura, no making a yule log with Laura, no picking out crackers to buy for the table. And certainly no discussing whether they'd be watching the Queen's speech or spending that time playing Clue.

Growing up, what Kit's family had lacked in money to spend on Christmas, they had made up for in time, spending hours planning and prepping for Christmas together.

Kit glared up at the cloudy, grey sky. There was definitely no holiday cheer this year, but what did it matter? It was only a few days at the end of the year. It shouldn't mean this much.

This is your first December in a new place, she reminded herself. *New job. New people. Everything has changed in your life this year. What you needed was a comfortable, safe, happy Christmas with some rituals you recognised. And to be with people who care about you.*

Kit shook off the melancholy and reminded herself once again that she wouldn't whinge. Then she opened the door to the library. Laura wanted to spend Christmas with her, and if she couldn't, she was going to make it up to her. That was the most comforting thought of all, because if there was one thing Kit knew, it was that Laura kept her promises.

Chapter Eight

TREACLE AND THE FROTHY VANILLA FRAPPE UNICORN FOAM

A few days later, the twenty-second of December turned up uninvited. Switching off her alarm, Kit blinked awake and stared at the date on her phone, questioning how it could be so close to Christmas. The twenty-second didn't seem to care. It had sat down and poured itself a cup of coffee. It was clearly here to stay.

There was also a text from Rajesh which said:

Siri, what's the weather? Remind me to ask Katherine about treacle. Oh, blooming heck, where are my trousers? Phyllis! Don't eat that, you stupid dog!

He'd clearly managed to get his mobile to dictate and then somehow sent it as a text. How? And why was he asking her about treacle? Was that even what he'd said? Kit shook her head as she, for the hundredth time, wondered why the world let Rajesh have a mobile phone.

She put her own phone down, flopped back on her pillow, and groaned. Three days until Christmas. At least they were closing the library after lunch on the twenty-fourth, so she only had a day and a half left of work. After that, she could spend all day reading in bed. Or celebrating Christmas if Laura was free. Kit began her increasingly habitual cursing that Laura did so much for Gage Farm and had wasted so much of December on the Christmas market, but then she stopped herself.

You fall in love with someone because of their big heart and then expect them to not give their every second doing stuff for others? Aimee's right, you're a plant pot.

Kit forced herself out of bed. She cleaned up, found some clothes, and headed towards the kitchen for some wake-up juice. After a big mug of tea and some banana porridge, she had just enough time for a couple of quick phone calls before she had to start walking to the library. She started with Laura, figuring that every day should start with hearing that warm, soft voice.

"Morning, dearest."

Kit leaned against the doorpost, happy butterflies in her stomach. "Hey, baby. Sleep well?"

"Not really, I got in late last night. There was a fight downtown and one of the Christmas market huts got damaged. Police Constable Sanders called me down there to assess the damage. I don't know why that couldn't wait until daytime, but you know what he's like."

"Yeah. Was everyone okay? What about the stall, I mean hut?"

"Some minor damage to the hut and to Rob Smith's face. PC Sanders said it could all be repaired in an hour or so. I think he was referring to the hut."

"Good. So that's why you couldn't see me last night?"

"Yes. Well, that and the fact that I had paperwork to do. I'm sorry."

Kit softly banged her head against the doorpost. "Don't apologise. I didn't mean to make you feel bad."

"You didn't. My lack of time for you did. It'll be better

after the holidays, I promise. After all, the Christmas market and the launch of our mulled wine will have been dealt with."

"True. The neglected paperwork will still be there, though, and the Stevensons will still be causing trouble."

"Yes, but that is everyday stuff which I can handle while still making time for you."

"Great. I look forward to it! Sorry for being so whingey. I finally figured out why; it's because it's my first Christmas away from my old life. Which, in combination with missing you, means I end up being miserable and clingy as a bleedin' puppy."

"I know, dearest," Laura said softly. "It's all such bad timing."

Kit ran her finger along the doorframe. "Also, 1 promised to help Shannon with something and I haven't been able to."

"Really? Another of your fixing-a-sticky-situation missions, is it? You haven't told me about that."

"No, there hasn't been time, and I was sworn to secrecy. Although, I'm sure she would be okay with telling you. Or wait, maybe I should ask her first. I need to text or call her before work for an update, I'll bring it up then. After all, you might have some insight that could help."

"I'll do anything I can to help even if it's merely being a sounding board."

The warmth of overwhelming affection tingled through Kit. "I know, honey. God, I miss you so much."

"I miss you excruciatingly much, too. So… should I let you get on with calling Shannon before you have to head into the library?"

Kit looked at her scuffed old fitness watch. "Bugger!

We've talked longer than I thought. I'm almost late! I need to get going."

"You mean you're still at home? I thought you were on your way to work?"

"No," Kit whimpered.

"Okay, stay there. I'll hop in the car, fetch you, and then drop you off at the library. You can ring Shannon as we drive?"

"Calling Shannon can wait. I can't ask you to pick me up, though, you're so busy."

"I can always take ten minutes out of my morning to drive my girlfriend to work. Get ready. I'll be there soon."

"Thanks," Kit said before hanging up.

She threw on her coat and boots, thanking fate for the fact that she lived on the same grounds where Laura worked. Meanwhile, she ignored the voice in the back of her head which pointed out that now she wasn't living in London with all its public transport, she should probably get her driving licence.

The mud-stained Volkswagen Beetle pulled up, and Kit hurried outside and into the car with a quick "good morning".

"Hi, lazy little sleep-in," Laura joked, claiming her hello kiss before driving off.

Then there were six glorious minutes of talking about what they'd dreamt and had for breakfast before they arrived at the library. Kit kissed her driver goodbye and promised to text or call at lunch.

"Have a great day. I love you, Kit Sorel."

"Ooh, using my full name?" she teased. "You must be serious."

"I am. I'm also parked here illegally, so get your fit

little bum into the library. I hope to hear from you at lunch."

"Count on it, my love. And remember, any free time you have, let me know. I'll pop in for a quick visit or stay the night or whatever we can manage."

"Absolutely. And I'll keep you posted about how things are looking for Christmas."

"You better. Especially as it is only days away."

There was a honk of a car behind Laura's. "Will do. Right, I better go. Speak soon, dearest."

"Bye, Laura."

Kit fished out her keys and began the procedure of unlocking the library, humming "It's Beginning to Look a Lot like Christmas" despite herself.

The clock struck twelve and Rajesh said, "Go for lunch, Katherine. When you come back, we need to talk about the table by the poetry section."

"*Table*? Aha. That makes a lot more sense than treacle. Remind me later."

He looked confused, but she had no time to explain about his weird dictated text. Her rush this morning meant she hadn't brought lunch or called Shannon. And of course, there was the call to Laura. Which took priority, as always.

She pulled her coat on and headed out into town to get some sandwiches and strong tea. Laura didn't answer her mobile, so Kit left a voicemail asking her to ring back. Then she tried Shannon, with better luck.

"Hi, Kit."

"Hey. You all right?"

"I'm fine. Really looking forward to Christmas now! I can't wait for all the holiday food and the presents. Rachel says she bought me something huge. You?"

Kit stopped to lean against a lamp post and hummed noncommittally.

"Ah, still haven't found your holiday cheer?"

"Nope," she said on an exhale. "Never mind all that, I was ringing to suggest I take a tiny break in the search for Pinky."

"Yeah, that makes sense," Shannon agreed.

"After the holidays I'll talk to Steve again and try to get the contact details for the woman he dated. Not that she sounded like the thieving type from what Steve said, but you never know who has a kleptomaniac streak deep down."

"Fair enough. To be honest, Rachel seems in a bit of a better mood. Maybe she's been distracted by all the holidays?"

"Could be. Either way, we'll get her favourite toy back after the holidays. Who knows, maybe Santa will bring it to her?"

Shannon scoffed. "I should hope not considering we're celebrating Christmas with both our families."

"Wow, sounds intense."

"It is. It'll be fun but crowded. It was actually my mum's idea. She's always been a bit uptight about the fact that I'm gay, so it's nice that she invited Rachel and her whole family for Christmas this year."

"Yeah! That's brilliant. I hope you'll have a lovely time. If I don't see you before then, Merry Christmas."

"I'm sure we'll see you around, but yeah, Merry Christmas!"

Kit said goodbye and hung up, realising that she

hadn't asked if it was okay for her to tell Laura about Pinky. Ah, well. That could wait.

Guided by her stomach, Kit headed for the café where she used to have lunch with Laura back when they were just friends.

She ordered a panini and a cup of tea and sat down. Her phone rang, and tingles coursed through Kit when she saw Laura's name on the screen.

"Hey, honey! Thanks for calling back."

"Hi, sorry I don't have long to talk. Obviously. I mean, what else is new?"

Kit hummed in agreement.

"But," Laura continued, "I wanted to quickly check in, while scoffing a huge slice of the yule log Tim brought for the office."

"Yum!"

"Yes. I think he feels guilty because he and the other employees haven't pitched in much lately. He said something about realising that even though I don't have kids I might still need to prepare for Christmas."

"That was nice of him," Kit muttered.

"His heart's in the right place. Also, this log is amazing. I'm rather sure my horrible, fat bottom agrees and that it's going to store the chocolaty goodness as insulated padding against these December winds."

"Laura, don't you dare call any part of yourself horrible. Your curves are amazing and I love them. Nevertheless, when all the stress is done, you do need to go back to eating food containing a vitamin or two for your health."

"Tell you what, when things ease up, I can go back to meeting you for lunch at Tea Gage, which I can hear you're at right now. I know the sound of that bell above the door."

"Yep, some of us are having a proper lunch. If I hitch-hike up to the Gage Farm office, I could bring you a sandwich and a cup of that frothy vanilla frappe unicorn foam you call coffee."

Laura sighed. "Thank you, but the Stevensons are arriving for a meeting in twenty minutes regarding the logo. I don't think they'll be happy to wait while I feast on sandwiches and the sight of a certain black-haired, pink-cheeked, blue-eyed beauty."

Kit squirmed and tried not to smile. "Aw, shucks. Well, stuff your face with that yule log and try to at least hydrate properly. Oh, and good luck with the Stevensons. Call me tonight?"

"I will. If it starts to get late and you haven't heard from me, please call me instead."

"Will do. I love you. Bye."

Just as Kit hung up, someone sat down at her table and roared, "You!"

Kit counted to ten in her head at the sight of Mabel Baxter. The island's best-known grammar enthusiast and complainer was currently pointing at Kit and scowling under her knitted hat.

"Hello, Mrs Baxter."

Mabel ignored the greeting. "Ethel informs me that you're lonely and therefore can't get into the Christmas spirit?"

"I suppose I—" Kit started to say before she was cut off.

"Well, young lady, I'm here to tell you that I have been a widow for more than ten years. Most of my friends are dead, and my family are all fools. The only person I have in my life is Ethel, who obviously celebrates Hanukkah.

Christmas is not a good time for me. Do you know what I did about that?"

Kit sat straighter, always feeling like a schoolgirl being told off when Mabel was around. "No?"

"I celebrate Hanukkah with Ethel and her son. Not because I've converted but because, in the end, it's not about the Christmas tree, the turkey, or even the presents. It's about you and the people you care about making a toast to having survived yet another year."

Kit cleared her throat. "Well, I would do that, but I'm not in contact with my mum, my dad is abroad, my best friend is celebrating on the mainland with her boyfriend's family, and my girlfriend doesn't even have time for lunch with me."

"Bah. Those aren't the only people in the world."

"Are you suggesting I come celebrate Hanukkah with you and Mrs Rosenthal? I will if it means finally getting to see what you look like under that hat," Kit said.

"Are you being facetious?" Mabel leered at her. "Never mind, I don't care. I simply came by to tell you to stop pitying yourself and to look around. You've made friends and acquaintances here. Ask them to spend the holidays with you. You don't need to find holiday cheer, you only need some company. And possibly a dry sherry to ward off the cold. Now eat and then get back to work."

With that, Mabel stood up and stomped off.

Kit was left gaping at the door. Then, she did as she was told and got back to her lunch, all while wondering if maybe she should ask Rach and Shannon, or Josh and Matt, if she could spend Christmas with them.

Chapter Nine

CHRISTMAS IS COMING. YOU CAN'T HIDE!

The twenty-fourth of December thudded down at Kit's feet like a rain-soaked package through the letterbox.

The only highlight of her time at work was a flurry of Christmas treats being dropped off throughout the day. Kit had been handed batches of homemade mince pies, tins of gingerbread, two Christmas puddings, and a box of chocolates from library regulars. One of the good things about Greengage's ageing population: most of them liked to bake and give away their baked goods.

When the library's closing procedures were taken care of, Rajesh held out his big hands. "I'll take the chocolates, Katherine. I'm going to spend the next few days catching up on my reading and could use the nibbles. You take all the fruity, spicy thingamabobs."

"Sure," Kit mumbled while stuffing gingerbread, mince pies, and the Christmas puddings into her rucksack and a plastic bag.

They parted with little fanfare, Rajesh going home to Phyllis and Kit popping into Steve's off-licence for some pouring cream to go with the mince pies and the puddings. At the last minute, she also picked up a bottle labelled as winter-spiced brandy.

Then she trudged through town and up the big hill, until she could see Howard Hall and knew she was minutes away from her little cottage. She'd go in, light those scented Christmas candles, break open the Gage Farm mulled wine again, and finish the bottle. After that, she could take a page out of Rajesh's book and catch up on some reading. She'd picked up a compilation of woman-loving-woman winter holiday stories, and it was waiting for her on her Kindle.

Then I'll call Aimee and guilt-trip her for leaving me alone on Christmas. No, that's not fair. She's got her own life on the mainland.

She could, however, call to see how Aimee and little George were doing and if she should ring them tomorrow to wish them a Merry Christmas.

She fished out her phone and located Aimee's number in her recent calls log.

"Hey, muppet," Aimee replied after the first ring.

"Hey, rude person. You all right?"

Aimee hummed. "Ups and downs over here. An 'up' is that our Christmas tree is bloody smashing this year! Oh, wait, George is pulling on my trouser leg. Wanna say something to your godmother, troublemaker?"

Kit heard scuffling as the phone was obviously handed over to the toddler.

A small voice coughed and then said, "Hi. What?"

Kit knew that "what?" was George speak for "guess what". Missing her best friend and this little bloke squeezed Kit's heart. "I've got no idea. Tell me."

"I drawn dinosaur. On wall."

Kit heard Aimee's gasp in the background and the thudding steps as she probably ran around checking the walls.

Trying not to laugh, Kit replied, "You're not allowed to do that, mate. Mummy is not going to be happy. I'd start looking very cute right about now if I were you."

"I cute all time."

"True. But you might want to ramp it up, sweetheart."

There were thudding steps as Aimee obviously returned. "George. Give me the phone and do not move, young man!"

Kit waited as she was once more handed over to her best friend.

"Hi again. I'm going to have to go," Aimee whinged. "I need to have a chat with George. And then scrub a wall." She groaned. "Or possibly *repaint* a wall."

"Right. I'll leave you to it. One thing before I do, though."

"Sure, shoot."

Kit rubbed the back of her neck. "Um, well, tomorrow's Christmas, right?"

"Yeah."

"Do you… think you might have time to ring me then?"

A moment of silence.

"Aw, love," Aimee said with a voice full of sympathy. "I promise you we'll talk tomorrow."

The vice-grip around Kit's heart loosened. "Great. Talk then. And good luck with the clean-up."

Aimee said goodbye and hung up.

Kit was left with only her Santa gnome for company. "Well, beardy. Now it's you, me, a bottle of the best mulled wine on the island, and some good reading material. Oh, and twenty thousand mince pies baked by every Greengager over fifty. Better get cracking!"

Her phone vibrated, revealing a text from Laura.

Hello dearest,
Something's wrong with the plumbing at Howard Hall. I'm trying to get a plumber who'll work today. Tom took a last-minute trip to London. Says he'll stay until the plumbing is fixed. I doubt I'll come over to yours tonight and I wouldn't recommend you come over here until I have this fixed. After I find a plumber I'm going back to the office to see if I can clear off some paperwork so I can take time off tomorrow. I'll keep you posted. I love you! Merry Christmas in advance.

Kit replied that she was sorry about the plumbing. She lamented the loss of their time together, but reassured Laura that she'd be at home and available whenever.

She had a long bath while drinking her first glass of mulled wine, then she got into her robe, got comfy on the sofa with her book, and munched on a couple of cold mince pies. When dinner came around, she had finished the book and was now sadder than ever. All those cute stories were about women spending the holidays with the ladies they loved. She ate a Christmas pudding for dinner just out of spite. It was an appropriate side dish to her bitterness, loneliness, and self-pity.

It was a quarter to nine, and Kit was still sitting on the sofa, warm in her fluffy robe and slippers in the shape of flamingos. By now she was also tipsy and queasy from only eating sugary treats. The telly was on, and she was trying to watch it without nodding off when the doorbell rang.

Kit rubbed her face.

I bet that's Mabel Baxter come here to tell me off for not having crashed someone's Christmas party.

She closed her robe tight to not scare off her visitor with her boobs. Or her depressed-and-no-sun-for-months pale skin.

When she opened the door, there was barely time to see who was on the other side since she was immediately assaulted with a huge hug.

Kit pushed her visitor away to greet her.

"Aimee! What the hell are you doing here?"

"First of all, is that how you greet friends who travelled during a holiday to this godforsaken island to see you? Secondly, why do you have flamingos on your feet? Thirdly, don't curse in front of my superb offspring, the Prince of Wall Painting."

Kit bent down, picked George up, and kissed his cold cheeks. She spun him round until they were both giggling.

Aimee laughed. "Can you two get out of the doorway and let me in? I'm freezing my ars—I mean, bum—off here."

Kit moved aside, still clinging onto George as if he might vanish if she let him go. "Of course. Hurry in! Blimey, I missed you two!"

"We missed you, too," Aimee said while lugging two big bags inside.

Kit took in the bags and her friend's red, puffy eyes. She put George down and said, "But missing me isn't the only reason why you're here, is it? Shouldn't you be with Mr Right?"

"Nope. He was Mr Wrong," Aimee said with a feeble

attempt at a smile. Then she crouched, opened a bag, and took out a bucket of Duplo. "George? Why don't you play with this for a while? Kit and I are going to pop into the kitchen for a chat."

He accepted the Duplo with open arms. "Yes!"

"Don't get too excited, though," Aimee warned. "It's way past your bedtime, so you'll have to go to sleep soon."

He nodded earnestly and toddled a few steps into the cottage before dropping unceremoniously to his bum and tugging open his Duplo bucket.

Kit followed Aimee into the snug kitchen. They were barely out of George's earshot before Aimee whispered, "I caught Carl telling George off for the wall painting."

"Okay? Is that a bad thing?"

"Not if he'd done it in a normal way. A non-screaming way. I'd talked to George earlier and made him understand that his wall art was wrong and denied him dessert as a punishment. George got it and has been an angel ever since. There was no need to shout at him for twenty minutes." Aimee pulled her hand through her long hair. "He really scared George, and not for the first time either. I've had to talk to Carl quite a few times about not disciplining George so hard and certainly not doing it without checking with me first."

"Seems like he didn't listen."

"Exactly. That shout fest was the straw that broke the camel's back. It doesn't matter how much I like a bloke, if he scares my son, I'm dumping him."

"So, no Christmas with Carl's family?"

"Nope." Aimee brightened. "Meaning that we were free to come to see you! Which, let's be honest, will be a hell of a lot more fun. Mind if we stay for a couple of days?"

"Are you kidding? Of course I don't bloody mind, love! I mean, I would've liked to know first, but hey, I don't mind a surprise if it's a nice one. I'll sleep on the sofa, and you and George can take the bed."

"Deal. I know you've had no holiday cheer, so I assumed the place would be Christmas free. I brought a few Santa ornaments to decorate with and some crackers to open. You know, to make it festive for George."

"Sure!" Kit glanced to the fridge. "I do have loads of mince pies, gingerbread, and a Christmas pudding, complete with pouring cream. Also, there's some holiday-themed brandy for you and me. But no turkey or sprouts or anything."

"That's okay. George and I mainly like the puddings anyway," Aimee said cheerfully.

Kit chewed her lower lip. It didn't feel right not to have a real Christmas with all the trimmings if she was going to have guests. Especially not if one of them was a child who was now celebrating away from home.

Aimee leaned in for a quick hug and said, "I should go get the little builder ready for bed. I'll be right back, and we can break into that brandy while I sob on your shoulder over my buggered relationship."

Kit kissed her hair. "It's a deal, mate. There are clean towels and stuff in the bathroom cupboards. Let me know if you need anything else."

"Will do," Aimee said as she went to gather up her son.

Kit stayed in the kitchen, trying to think of ways to arrange a full holiday celebration for her guests.

For the first time this month, it felt like there was going to be a real Christmas.

And for the first time this month, Kit wasn't pitying

herself. At least not as long as she didn't think about Laura's absence.

Anyway. Maybe a tin of chicken soup can serve as a turkey substitute?

Kit started rummaging around the kitchen with new energy.

Chapter Ten

CHRISTMAS DAY KISSES

The next morning it happened. The twenty-fifth of December arrived right when the calendar said it should. Christmas Day's arrival was heralded by George jumping up on Kit's stomach to give her his usual rousing: a wet kiss on the nose.

Kit pushed her slight hangover aside and gave him a cuddle. "Ah! I missed those morning nose kisses of yours, Georgie. Merry Christmas. You sleep okay?"

He nodded while patting her head. "Yes. Your hairs are pointy. Comb it."

"I will, mate. I need to wake up first, though. Is your mum awake?"

Another nod. "Shower."

"Good. Let's get some tea and toast on the go."

"Present?"

"Nope, no Christmas gifts yet, mate."

"Okay," he said with a shrug. He jumped off her to run toward the kitchen.

"Don't know why you're rushing, kid. You can't reach the kettle or the toaster," Kit muttered as she dragged herself off the sofa. She found herself smiling despite the sleepiness and hangover from the mulled wine and brandy last night.

I'm not alone for Christmas.

She kept her duvet on as a cape as she switched the heating on and then went into the kitchen. While she was filling the kettle, her phone vibrated on the counter. She blinked at the screen and saw a text from Laura.

Good morning, my love. Oh, and Merry Christmas! I found a plumber yesterday and he fixed the problem. I think the smell is gone, but I can't tell anymore. Can you come over in a while and check for me?

Kit frowned but texted back that she'd be over when she was dressed and fed, with a quick mention that Aimee and George had come over for a few days. By the time she finished the text by saying she loved Laura, the frown was clearly gone, as George looked at her and said, "Kit happy?"

She bent down to ruffle his hair. "I will be when I've had some tea. Move over, young kitchen assistant. I think I have some cereal puffs you'd like."

❧

After breakfast, Aimee and George were cuddled up on the sofa watching Christmas shows, so Kit got cleaned up and ambled over to Howard Hall.

Her breath steaming and crows cawing to welcome the Christmas morning, Kit wondered if her girlfriend had meant for her to use her spare key or if Laura would be there to check for smells with her. She hoped for the latter with such force that she marched to the tall Edwardian door in record time.

She rang the doorbell and waited.

And waited.

And waited some more.

With a sigh, she gave up and reached for the keys in her pocket. Right then the door opened. Kit expected to see her girlfriend but was instead faced with a familiar short, plump woman with two layers of makeup. Maybe three. Mrs Imelda Smith, Howard Hall's part-time cook, smelled of sprouts and sherry this morning. Hopefully that was due to her cooking and not what she'd had for breakfast.

Kit took a step back. "Oh! Hello, Mrs Smith."

"Hello, lass. Happy Christmas." Mrs Smith threw a huge coat over her shoulders and said, "Well, I'm off. I have my own Christmas dinner to see to now." Her face broke into a grin. "Would ya thank Laura for the bonus for me? I reckon I was too blown away to say 'ta'. I'll be taking the family to Tenerife next year with that sort of cash! Cheerio."

She stomped off, leaving Kit with a "Merry Christmas" on her lips. She shook her head and stepped inside, calling, "Laura?"

"Coming!" her honeyed voice called from upstairs. "Hang on. Don't come inside! Wait until I'm down."

Kit dutifully stepped back out. Before she did, she picked up delicious smells of open fires, some sort of sweet spice, and oranges, all congregating in the air of the old building.

Laura strode down the stairs. In one jolt, all breath left Kit's body.

Laura wasn't wearing her usual work attire or even the comfier clothes she sometimes wore around the house. She was wearing a red dress which hugged her body almost indecently tight, putting every curve on display. A fine film of black lace decorated the front of the dress. Laura's hair was up in a bun with a few curls hanging down to frame her face in a casual but clearly deliberate way. Her makeup was perfect, and her legs were sheathed in a pair of sheer, black tights. Or maybe stay-ups. Kit's mind was too blown to even dare guess. Finishing the ensemble was a pair of black pumps with impressively high heels.

Kit watched her descend the stairs, still breathless but with a heart that was working overtime.

So this is how I die, huh? Fair enough.

When her eyes found Laura's, she noticed her usually insecure and self-deprecating girlfriend wearing a knowing little smirk.

"I take it you like my outfit?"

"L-like it? I want to bloody well marry it! Look at *you*." Kit made a sound somewhere between a sob and a sigh. "You look like, I don't know, all the good things in the world. But even better!"

She cursed emphatically and was grateful George wasn't with them. Not only because of the cursing, but because her mind was painting images of what she wanted to do to Laura when she got her out of that dress. Suddenly the air seemed heavy with lust.

Laura took her hand and pulled her into the house, her smirk growing into a beaming smile. No one could embody the word *beam* like Laura.

"God, I've missed you, Kit. So much that I had to take action. I've put all paperwork aside over the holidays and told the Stevensons and everyone else that I'm out of communication. Even for emergencies."

"Really? That's amazing news! When did you decide that?"

"Two days ago. I was working and suddenly began missing you as if I hadn't seen you for years. All while you were only a few minutes' walk away. So, I started planning to give you the perfect Christmas. I was going to ask you over yesterday, but I wasn't quite finished getting the tree up."

Kit squeezed her hand. "Hence the plumber story?"

Laura bit her lip. "Yes. You caught me. I'm sorry, I hated lying to you. I only wanted everything to be perfect for our first Christmas together."

Kit took her eyes and attention off of Laura for a second. The Christmas smells were even stronger now. Some wafted in from the kitchen downstairs, while others came from the drawing room where a fire was lit and a huge tree took centre stage.

"Whoa! Look at that. George will love it." Kit's head snapped back to Laura. "Ah. You planned all this not knowing that Aimee and George were coming. Sorry."

"No need to apologise! I simply made a few alterations to the plans. I had bought you a naughty Mrs Claus outfit to wear, but that will have to wait until it's just us. Other than that, everything can be changed to incorporate them. After all, they lived here for a while, they're basically family."

"Speaking of family, I'm guessing what you said about Tom was true?"

"Yes, but he didn't leave because of plumbing issues. I paid for him to get some winter sun, and he happily—"

"Buggered off," Kit interjected.

"I was going to say 'vanished in an instant', but yes."

Laura suddenly leapt and giggled. Kit looked down and realised that her fingers were snaking around Laura's waist, clearly tickling her.

What? My hands are perving without even involving my brain now? Bloody hell, was I that Laura-deprived? Well, yes, silly question.

"I'm so sorry, baby. I really didn't notice I'd started touching you."

"Well, now that you have…" Laura lowered her voice. "Why don't you touch something a little more… sensitive?"

Kit grabbed a handful of Laura's bum and growled deep in her throat. In response, Laura kissed her. Kit found herself forgetting all about the wonderful surprise, Aimee and George back in the cottage, the Christmas tree, the food smells from the kitchen, and even Laura's delicious outfit. All she could think about was how good Laura felt and how much she needed her.

Clearly on the same page, Laura broke away and whispered, "Come upstairs, dearest. The plans can wait."

"Aimee and George will wonder where I am."

"We'll be quick. We only need enough to take the edge off. The real lovemaking will be tonight."

"Oh," Kit paused to lick Laura's lower lip, "will it now?"

"Yes," Laura growled. "I wasn't joking about the sexy Mrs Claus outfit. One of us is wearing it tonight and the other is going to get to take it off, using only her teeth."

"Count me in," Kit purred. "But a quickie first, I'm dying here."

Laura took her hand, and they rushed upstairs to start the Christmas celebration by unwrapping each other.

છે.

That afternoon, while Aimee and George watched the Queen's speech, Kit stood down in Howard Hall's suddenly more decorated kitchen with Laura, even though she was so full from the lunch that she never wanted to see another kitchen in her life. They'd just gone over the checklist of all the food for the rest of the day, including the puddings that they'd picked up from the cottage while fetching Aimee and George.

Kit blew out a breath. "Wow. The feast continues then. That's a lot of food."

"The way you exercise, dearest, you'll work it off soon enough," Laura said as she inspected Tupperware boxes of parsnips, sprouts, and carrots.

Kit checked out the decorations. The holly above the stove seemed to have spread to the rest of the kitchen, while red baubles painted with black snowflakes hung from the ceiling light. They matched Laura's dress perfectly.

It was all perfect. The Christmas which Kit had been dreading was now shaping up to be one of the best of her life. Still, it wasn't quite right. She wasn't lonely anymore, but she knew someone who was.

"Babe?"

"Yes?" Laura replied while opening the lid on a huge saucepan that was simmering away on the stove.

"Would you mind if I invited one more person?"

"What? No, of course not. Goodness knows we have enough room and food. Mrs Smith has gone a bit overboard, bless her. Who did you have in mind?"

Kit shoved her hands into the pockets of her chinos. "Rajesh."

"Oh. I didn't think he celebrated Christmas?"

"He doesn't. However, he's not overly religious, and whether or not he's willing to admit it, I think he'd rather be with us while we celebrate than be alone."

Laura tilted her head. "I don't know, dearest. I love you for worrying about him, but… Rajesh usually likes to either be on his own or be romancing a lady. A family holiday, especially one he doesn't celebrate, doesn't sound like his sort of event."

"I know." Kit looked up at the holly above. "Still, I can't shake the feeling that he didn't really want to be alone this time. When we closed the library yesterday, he seemed like he wanted to drown his sorrows in chocolate more than enjoy his beloved alone time." She gazed back to Laura. "I won't be able to relax until I've at least offered that he should join us."

Laura kissed her tenderly. "All right, dearest. Go make the call. Whether he accepts or not, send him my love."

Kit went upstairs, mobile in hand, to get a signal. After a few rings, she heard Phyllis barking in the background and Rajesh telling her to shush.

"Hey there, boss man."

"Katherine. Hello. What's that racket in the background?"

"The Queen's speech mixed with Aimee's little George singing "Last Christmas". I'm at Howard Hall. Laura surprised me by arranging a Christmas celebration. Before that, Aimee and George surprised me by coming to stay for a few days."

Rajesh grunted. "That's a lot of surprises. What's wrong with people?"

"I don't know," Kit said, stifling a laugh. "I think they

did it because they like me and wanted to stop me from moping around."

"I suppose," he muttered.

"Anyway, I was wondering…"

"Yes?"

"I know you don't celebrate Christmas and that you were hoping to catch up on your reading, but I, well, I miss you. And Aimee, George, and Laura are all nearly as crazy about you as I am. Is there any way we can convince you to pop in for a while?"

"Katherine…"

"Wait, hear me out. You wouldn't have to take part in anything Christmassy. It would be like a nice, non-religious dinner with friends. There's loads of food, including parsnips which look like they've been drowned in butter and honey. I know you love them."

There was a grunt on the line. "Katherine, some people like to be alone."

"Of course," Kit replied, regret making her squirm. "I know that lots of people truly enjoy being alone, whether it's a holiday or not. I get that, and I respect it. If you don't wanna come, then I'll leave you be. I only wanted—"

"No," Rajesh barked. "I'll come. For your sake. And because Phyllis needs to be taken out for a walk anyway. Are there chocolates?"

Kit's heart lifted. "Loads. Laura bought really fancy brands."

"Fine. Don't eat them until I get there. Also, you have to make sure young George doesn't pull the hair in my ears again."

"Consider it done," Kit chirped.

"Good. I'll be there around five. I have a book to finish."

"Great. I'll see you and Phyllis then. Laura sends her love, she—"

Kit was cut off by the fact that Rajesh had hung up. She chuckled as she put away the phone and went to join Laura in the kitchen.

Chapter Eleven

IT'S BEGINNING TO LOOK A LOT LIKE CHRISTMAS

The clock struck five, signalling that they were now an hour away from Christmas dinner. Kit wasn't sure where the hell she was going to find room in her full stomach for it, but, considering how great everything smelled, she was willing to figure it out.

The doorbell rang, and Kit raced Aimee to the door with George at their heels. Kit won and opened the door for Rajesh. Phyllis caught sight of George and stormed straight in to greet the boy with a face-licking he'd never forget. He laughed and tried to hug the overweight, overexcited mutt.

Meanwhile, Kit and Aimee invited Rajesh in and took turns giving him hugs.

He had a bag in one hand and was holding it awkwardly out of sight.

"What's in there?" Aimee asked.

Rajesh shuffled his feet. "A couple of toys for Phyllis, a hat for if it's colder when I walk home, and… well, I made some naan. I know it's not for Christmas, but I wanted to contribute, and while people don't appreciate my curries, everyone seems to like my naan bread."

After closing the door behind him, Aimee peered into the bag. "You could say that we like your naans," she said. "Or we could be honest and say that we bloody well love them!"

"And," Kit added, "that any food you bring, particularly if it's something that makes you feel at home, is appreciated."

"Especially if it's not icky sprouts or dry turkey," Aimee retorted with a grin. "Thanks for making something special."

He scowled at her and said under his breath, "Well, you four have all become pretty special to me."

Kit wanted to thank him and fuss over him for being so sweet, but she knew he'd hate it. Aimee, as always, had less self-restraint. At least she stuck to only patting his shoulder and softly saying, "I wish I could meet a bloke like you. But, you know, younger, less hairy, and less likely to seduce every woman over fifty."

He rolled his eyes at her and went to extract his dog from the toddler, who was now trying to blow a raspberry into the dog's fur.

"Come away from the child, Phyllis. You'll knock him over. Here, have something to play with."

He fished out a toy from the bag. Phyllis took it and began chewing on it with her tail wagging.

Kit stared at the toy and began laughing hysterically.

Aimee, George, Rajesh, and Phyllis all stared at her.

"Kit? Has your brain mushed into Christmas pudding?" Aimee asked.

"Woof?" Phyllis added around the gnawed toy.

Kit cleared her throat. "I'm fine. I, um, just have to ask… where did you get that, Rajesh?"

"What? The toy Phyllis is chomping on? She found it when we were out one day. Probably in the park." He took his coat off as he added, "She chewed it beyond recognition right away, so I can't say what it's meant to be, some sort of squeaky toy shaped as a bone I suppose? Why?"

Kit fought back more laughter. Why Rajesh would say 'beyond recognition' was understandable when you saw the thing Phyllis was chewing. Kit, however, took in what looked like a hole for batteries, the bright pink colour, the phallus shape, and knew that she had found Pinky.

"Oh, nothing," she croaked. "I thought it was something else. Why don't you all get comfy in to the drawing room? I'll be with you soon. I've got a call to make."

They strode off, taking Phyllis and the destroyed Pinky with them.

Kit got her phone out and called Shannon, laughter still bubbling up inside her.

"Merry Christmas, Kit," Shannon's husky voice boomed.

"Same to you. I'm gonna skip the pleasantries here and get straight to the important news."

"Okay," Shannon said apprehensively. "Which is?"

"I found Pinky."

"What?"

"Yep. That's the good news. The bad news is who the thief is."

"Who?!"

"Phyllis. She's been using it as a chew toy, clearly ever since she and Rajesh visited your house."

"Bugger, crap, bollocks." There was a thud as if

Shannon had hit or kicked something. "Hm. Sorry about that. So, does, uh, does Rajesh know what it is?"

"Do you really think he'd let his dog play with it if he did?"

"No, fair point. Good thing I had taken the batteries out of it before I washed it. I wouldn't want Phyllis to have eaten batteries." Shannon paused to blow out a long breath. "Well, I guess that's the end of Pinky then."

"As a sex toy? Yes. As a dog toy, its life carries on," Kit replied.

"Not much of a relief."

"I guess not. Later on, I'll explain to Rajesh what it is and throw Pinky away since I'm not sure it's safe to be chewed. How are you going to—"

Kit had been about to ask Shannon how she would break it to Rachel when she heard the woman in question in the background, asking, "Who's that on the phone, hot stuff?"

Shannon made a comical gulping noise.

"Tell her the truth," Kit whispered into the phone. Then she stood back against the wall, unsure of if she should be listening or not, while Shannon told Rachel all.

Kit could hear high-pitched laughter in the background. Then the laughter turned into distorted words sounding like, "You thought I was upset over the dildo? Babe, it's only a toy."

"Then what were you upset about?" asked Shannon.

Kit couldn't help but strain her ears to hear Rachel's answer.

"Christmas and your mum. You know how she feels about you being gay, and that bleeds through to how she feels about me. The second she invited not only us, but also my entire family, over for Christmas, months of anxiety lifted off my shoulders. I thought you knew that."

"Christ," Shannon groaned. "That makes so much more sense. I thought it was because of Pinky. You said that it was the perfect size and shape and that we couldn't replace it."

"I did say that, and I was upset. However, it was the worry about your mum that made me overly sensitive to everything that went wrong, including Pinky's disappearance."

"Oh," Shannon said softly.

Kit heard Rachel laugh again and add, "Don't worry about Pinky being gone. It only means that we have to buy—and try out—loads of toys until we find the perfect replacement. It might be a bit pricey, but it'll also be so much fun."

The tone in Rachel's voice made Kit decide it was time for her to extract herself from the conversation. "Um, right, so that's the mystery solved then," she said.

"Huh? Kit, sorry, mate, obviously you don't want to listen to all this. You're right about the mystery. Thanks so much for the help! Tell you what, would it be all right if Rachel I and pop over with some treats tomorrow night? To thank you and to catch up."

"Sure, as long as you bring enough for Aimee and George, who're staying with me. And possibly for Laura, too, as she's taken time off."

"Really? That's smashing. Looks like your Christmas worked out nicely, then?"

Kit thought of the lonely, uncertain holiday season she had expected and then overlaid the image of Aimee, George, Rajesh, Laura, and herself, with all the food, gorgeous decorations, and no doubt wonderful presents to come.

"Yeah. Not to be corny, but I kinda got my own little Christmas miracle."

"Glad to hear it, mate. You deserve it." There was a whisper on the line before Shannon came back. "I have to go. Rachel says that her dad is hitting on my nan. We've got to intervene. Have a great Christmas day. I'll see you tomorrow."

"See you then," Kit agreed. "Good luck with the intervening. Give my love to Rachel and Merry Christmas to all of you."

"Same to you. Bye."

Kit hung up and stuck her phone back into the pocket. Clacking steps on the hallway's stone floor behind her scared her half to death.

"Bloody hell, Laura," she exclaimed. "Warn a person that you're there."

Laura invaded her personal space with an apologetic grimace. "Sorry. Warning: I'm here. Second warning: I overheard parts of that conversation and am now thoroughly confused. What is a Rinky and how can it be both a sex toy and a dog toy?"

Kit ran her hand over her face, trying to brush the embarrassment off it. "Pinky, not Rinky." She then started telling the sad tale of Pinky.

When she had finished, Laura crossed her arms over her chest with a smirk. "A vibrating strap-on, huh? I've never had much interest in strap-ons. After all, I dated men before you and they didn't have much need for them." Her face fell. "Unless they wanted me to use one on them? Oh. Maybe I should have asked? Do you think

Dylan would have been happier in our relationship if I... what's the word..."

Kit ran her hand over her face again, harder this time. "Pegged him. And no, I don't. I also don't want to think about your ex."

"Oh, don't worry. He and my aunt are still happily playing house in the South of France. He won't bother us."

"I know, baby. I've read all the postcards with you, remember?" Kit said tenderly. "Now, would you mind getting back to your point?"

"Pardon? Oh. Right, I'm babbling again, aren't I?"

Kit leaned in and kissed her forehead. "Yes. And while it's as adorable as always, did you have something to say about strap-ons?"

"I did! I was saying that I never much cared for them. Although now that I know they can vibrate, well... you know how I feel about things that vibrate."

Kit grinned as she recalled Laura's shocked face when she'd shown her the toy box hidden under her bed. She also recalled that after trying them out, it was obvious that Laura's favourites were the ones that vibrated. *All* of the ones that vibrated.

Suddenly it felt like years ago that they had managed that quickie upstairs.

Laura made a pitying sound, clearly not reading Kit's expression as one of lust and need. "This isn't the time for sex talk, is it?" she asked. "Your beautiful cheeks have gone from their normal pink to bright Christmas red."

Laura combed her fingers through Kit's hair, sighed, and whispered, "I love your hair. It's getting long in the back, though. We need to get you a hair appointment. Unless you're growing it out?"

Kit leaned into the touch. "Nope. Unless you'd like me to?"

Laura kept running her fingers gently through the strands. "Your hair would be perfect any way you wanted to wear it, although, I have to say, I like it short. Like it was when you first moved to the island."

"I'll go get it cut. *After* we get to enjoy all that alone time you promised," Kit said before stealing a quick kiss.

"Count on it. For the rest of this holiday season, I'm not letting you farther than a hair's breadth from me," Laura said, playfully tugging on a few tresses.

"Oi! Lovebirds! Are you coming back in here or have you eloped?" Aimee called from the drawing room.

"We better join them," Kit whispered, nuzzling her nose against Laura's.

They strolled in, hand in hand. Aimee was nodding her head in time to "It's Beginning to Look a Lot Like Christmas" while inspecting the contents of a chocolate box. Rajesh and George were fussing over Phyllis.

"I have to keep her away from the tree," Rajesh explained. "She either wants to play with it or pee on it. Or possibly eat it." He spotted their intertwined hands. "Should we leave you two alone? I know you've been struggling to get time together lately."

"It's fine," Laura assured him. "After this holiday there'll be no more Christmas market and no new mulled wine to promote. Plus, I'll try to delegate more of the paperwork and the constant emergencies to my employees, meaning Kit and I can have some quality time together."

"Nice. Going on a cheeky holiday?" Aimee mumbled through a mouth full of Godiva chocolate.

Laura turned to Kit with eyebrows raised in question.

Kit shook her head. "Nah, I think we'll stay here. Or

at the cottage if Tom comes back to haunt this place. Let's not waste time travelling. I just want two full weeks of kissing."

"Makes sense," Aimee said before swallowing her chocolate and adding, "You know, if you don't want a repeat of this year's separation next Christmas, why don't you join the events committee, too?"

"Excellent idea," Rajesh said with a mischievous grin.

Laura almost hid her snigger as she said, "Yes, then you can help with the inevitable Christmas market next year."

Kit put her hands on her hips and looked at the teasing faces of her makeshift little family. "If you muppets think I'm going to join the events committee which invented 'kitten races,' you're all bonkers."

Rajesh picked up a glass of Gage Farm mulled wine and held it up in a toast. "Here's to 'bonkers'. I'll take it over Christmas spirit or holiday cheer any day."

They all found their glasses and toasted to that.

AUTHOR'S NOTE

Thanks for reading!

If you enjoyed this story and want to read more about Kit and Laura (and understand more about the quirky inhabitants of Greengage and the island's weird history) purchase a copy of the first book in the series *Greengage Plots* or read on for an exclusive preview of the first three chapters of the upcoming sequel *Greengage Shelf.*

(Note that this book includes footnotes, if you're reading on an ebook then you can click the small number next to text where displayed. If you're reading a paperback, flip to the end of the segment for a list of endnotes.)

GREENGAGE SHELF PREVIEW

Greengage Shelf

EMMA STERNER-RADLEY

Chapter One

RHINOS AND RELUCTANT DETECTIVES

K it frowned at a speck of mud on her jeans. It was in the exact shape of a rhino. She wiped at it, obviously just smearing the rhino into a huge blob. This was all her fault. Well, mostly her fault.

If she hadn't agreed to sort out the matter of Widow Caine's books, they wouldn't be in a muddy ditch right now. Or rather, they wouldn't be if she hadn't made them leave the cottage in that ridiculous way. Kit was aware of that. She was also aware of Laura sighing, quietly but demonstratively.

Kit's girlfriend, Laura, was a sweet soul who would never blame or harangue her for taking this little mystery on. Be that as it may, Laura clearly wasn't happy about her expensive dress being muddy while her favourite heeled boots had switched from their original, stylish grey to mud brown.

Kit got up, adjusted her glasses, and held out a hand to her girlfriend. Laura took it and stood. Other than the look of annoyance, there were also flecks of mud on Laura's face, almost blending in with her freckles. The difference being that the freckles were half-hidden by make-up while the mud stood tall and proud on those soft cheeks.

"You know, this isn't *only* my fault," Kit tried. "If you hadn't asked for the recipe for the shortbread, we probably wouldn't be here. We'd have gone home long before this all kicked off and left in a normal way no less."

"That's true, dearest."

That was all her girlfriend said. The silence spoke the rest.

What had brought them to this damn ditch in the first place was a visit to Widow Caine's cottage on Nettle Road to start off the investigation. Because Kit had solved a few tricky situations on the island of Greengage since she arrived a year ago, she'd been asked to look into a mystery regarding some books that had been moved around in the widow's home—and one that had been stolen.

They'd gone to Nettle Road right after Laura finished up at the office of her family fruit farm[1] and picked Kit up from her job at the library. When they arrived, they were told the whole tale of how the books had been neatly arranged one day, then moved about, and then moved about again. Finally, one had gone missing. A copy of *Journey to the Centre of the Earth* by Jules Verne, to be exact.

Kit remembered reading it as a teenager but had no clue if she had liked it. That was back in the day when she tried to wow the other girls with her speed reading. The result was that none of them were impressed and that Kit had read loads of books she didn't remember anything about. Had there been a moose in this one? Or was that some other book?

Telling them the whole mysterious tale over shortbread

and weak tea was the owner of the books and the cottage, Widow Caine herself.

Kit clicked her tongue as she inwardly scolded herself. *I have to remember to call her Alice. Not "Widow Caine" like people do on this island, which is still stuck in the forties. No wait. The twenties. Or maybe it's in completely its own time period. Possibly a parallel universe.*

After Alice told them the story, she divulged that the only suspects, meaning those who had visited the cottage around the time that the Verne book was stolen, were:

Phillip Caine. Alice Caine's oldest son at fifty-four years of age. A former Wing Commander in the Royal Air Force. He was retired now due to a back injury, which left him in chronic pain.

Jacqueline "Jackie" Caine. Alice Caine's daughter-in-law. Aged forty-five. She'd been a theatre costume designer back in her native Edinburgh. She quit her job and moved to Greengage when she married Phillip in the late nineties.

Anthony Caine. Alice Caine's youngest son at forty-nine years old. Formerly living in Devon but returned to Greengage two months ago, after losing his job as an architect.

Caitlin Caine. Alice Caine's youngest grandchild. Aged thirteen. The only of a sibling group of three to not only still live with her parents, Phillip and Jackie, but to remain in Britain. Her older brothers both live abroad. According to her grandmother, Caitlin "needs a spot of attention."

Liam Soames. Alice Caine's neighbour. Twenty years old. Known to the police but has lately been "improving his ways."

Liam, while not a family member, did odd jobs like mowing the lawn and, recently, mending the fence. He had a spare key, just like Alice's two sons. Jackie and

Caitlin would have been able to access those keys as well, of course. Liam's key, however, was to the backdoor.

All that information had been great. So had the shortbread. Their exit, on the other hand, was decidedly not. They had needed to leave in a rush, out through the window. This was due to a knock and a booming voice saying, "Mother? Let me in. Jackie has my key," which indicated that suspect number one—Phillip, who Alice regretfully admitted was her main suspect due to his refusal to let her investigate the bookshelf mystery—was at the door.

It had been Kit's idea to jump out the window. That way, Wing Commander Caine wouldn't know his mother had asked someone to look into the missing book affair. At the time, diving through the window had seemed like a fun way to add a little action to the venture. Except, outside of that particular window was a steep slope, which led to a muddy, roadside ditch. The one which she and Laura were now wearing as a crusting shell over their clothes. Kit knew that Laura would've suggested they tell Phillip that they'd only popped in for tea or something, if Kit hadn't jumped out that window with the *Mission Impossible* theme playing in her head first.

At least Widow Caine had been happy that they left with such stealth, whispering out the window that it made her happy to see them taking it so seriously.

Alice. Her name is Alice, you numpty.

Kit looked back at the cottage. "Isn't it weird that even Rajesh calls Alice 'Widow Caine?' I mean, they're the same age, and he even dates her on and off, doesn't he?"

"I'm not sure 'date' is the correct term, dearest."

Kit snorted. That was how a posh, well-brought-up person like Laura would say that Rajesh, Kit's boss at the library and her former landlord, slept with every eligible woman over sixty on Greengage.

Laura picked up again. "But yes, it is odd that no one uses her first name. Another one of those old-fashioned habits Greengage clings to that you always laugh about, I suppose."

Kit winced. *There's the offended voice. How do I smooth this over?*

"Babe, if I ever laugh at Greengage and Greengagers, it's the way you can giggle at your family members. You still love and respect them even if they're acting silly."

Laura was dragging her fingers through her bouncy curls, trying to get some mud flecks out. "Family members? Does that mean you finally feel at home here?"

"Yeah. I mean, I'll always be a Londoner. That's the way I was raised." Kit scanned the quiet, leafy street. "Still, this sort of feels like home. Like… a new home."

"New? You've lived here for more than a year."

"I don't mean 'new home' as in that I've recently moved here." Kit adjusted her glasses while thinking of how to explain what she meant. "It's more like if you've grown up in a house and moved to a flat. It takes a long time to get your subconscious used to it. Everything is different, but with time, it starts to become your natural base."

Images of her little cottage popped into her head, and sure enough, that feeling in her chest was the safety and comfort of home. And the knowledge that she'd filled the place with books and posh teas. No more sticking to one bookshelf due to cramped London apartments; no more sticking to regular tea due to high London prices.

Meanwhile, Laura had retrieved a pack of tissues from her pocket and was using one to wipe at her dress. She scowled at the mud and put the filthy tissue back in her pocket. "Never mind. I'll get it dry-cleaned next time I'm on the mainland," she said with a brave smile.

"I promised Dad I'd go to London to see him soon," Kit said. "We can have it dry-cleaned then."

Laura gave her a quick kiss. "I'm sure that will be fine. Let's head back to the car."

Her little Volkswagen Beetle had been parked at the bottom of Nettle Road. That was one thing which was the same in London as here on this island. Never enough parking.

"Anyway, what do you make of your little case, Miss Marple?" Laura teased as they walked.

"I'm hardly a Miss Marple, or any other kind of detective, for that matter." Kit paused to groan. "This is really not my thing. I'm a librarian. Sure, I help friends figure out if their boyfriends are cheating on them and solve people's money issues, but I don't unearth missing things. Not even books."

"Missing *book*," Laura corrected gently. "Only *Journey to the Centre of the Earth* has been taken, remember?"

"Mm. If we're taking Alice Caine's word for that it's actually gone."

Laura furrowed her brow. "Why shouldn't we?"

"Well, I mean, she's not young. She might be getting confused or forgetful. Or maybe her loneliness has her making up stories to get company and attention?"

"Widow Caine is sharp as a whip and certainly not lonely. Yes, she misses her late husband, but she still has friends. Not to mention her children and grandchildren."

Kit shoved her hands into the pockets of her leather-jacket. "Mm. True."

Laura shot her a glance. "Are you sure you want to wear that?"

"What? I always wear this jacket. Unless its freeze-your-bum-off winter."

"Yes, but darling, it's summer."

Kit noticed she was picking up the walking pace. "It's a cold day. And only June."

"Cold? Dearest, it's 22 degrees."

She stopped to make eye contact with her girlfriend. "Hey! This jacket with my vintage blue Converse is… my signature outfit."

Laura watched her from under those long, mascara-clad eyelashes. "Do you need a signature outfit, my love? Is it part of your detective lark, now? Like Sherlock Holmes' deerstalker or Hercule Poirot's moustache?"

Kit wanted to play along with the banter, but she didn't have a proper comeback. She didn't want to be the island's famous detective. She did, however, want to wear her jacket. Even if she was beginning to sweat a little.

Laura almost managed to hide a smile. "Still, it does make you stunningly sexy. Now, get in the car so we can have a shower and something cool to drink before dinner."

"Great idea! Remind me to wash my Converse first."

"Sure. You're lucky that your shoes can go in the washing machine. My boots look ruined."

While Laura mumbled something about having the car's interior cleaned later, they got in the car and drove up the hill up to Gage Farm and the adjacent Howard Hall, Laura's family home. On its grounds was the old work-man's cottage Kit was renting from her. *Home.*

The smell of mud made Kit open the car window. Somewhere in the trees a bird sang as if it were really trying to tell them something. Or trying to woo a partner, perhaps? Animals were still a bit of a mystery for a Londoner like Kit. Unless the animal in question was a pigeon or a rat. They mostly just wanted to not get run over. Or a chance to steal your chips.

Kit spotted Mrs Morney, who lives about five houses down the road. She was walking her sausage dog at a pace not much faster than a hungover snail. She and the dachshund turned and began walking home again. Kit heard the old lady say, "That's enough, Bronwyn. You've had your long walk today already. We won't go all the way to the square this time."

Kit made a mental note of that as she considered whether or not to inform Rajesh. After all, she had to protect her investments in their new hobby of dog walking bets.

She leaned back and thought about borrowing some clean clothes after the shower with her girlfriend. And about what might drive someone to steal a book.

---

1. The famous Gage Farm. Read *Greengage Plots* for more info. Or keep reading this book. One mustn't let footnotes dictate reading habits.

Chapter Two

UPDATING RAJESH

The next day, Kit peered out at the crowded library. It was nice to see the place so packed, even if most of the people weren't there for the books but to hear a famous naval hero called Admiral Warshaw speak about his brave adventures at sea. That talk was scheduled for 3:30 p.m. It was 11:00 a.m. now and the library was full of elderly Greengagers, all with a glint in their eye. The men, who were in the minority, were buzzing about hearing Warshaw's thrilling tales of combat and survival at sea. The ladies were all buzzing about handsome sailors and the fact that they had never seen an actual admiral before.

Kit wished they'd stop asking her when he would arrive and if their newly blue-rinsed hair looked nice.

Rajesh appeared at her side, patting his big belly to the tune of "Rule, Britannia." "So. Next Sunday, my money will be on Honoria Shaw. I took her out to dinner last night, and she said her Pekingese, Mewly, is in heat and needs loads of walking."

"Why is Mrs Shaw's dog called Mewly?"

Kit instantly regretted asking the man who'd named his bulldog mix *Phyllis* a question like that.

"Dunno. Perhaps it mewls? It's always locked in the kitchen when I call on Honoria."

Oh, so it's Honoria now, huh? It used to be Mrs Shaw. Looks like Romeo here has a new favourite.

She squeezed her lips together to not smirk at him. "Either way, your bet is on Mewly and Mrs Shaw, then? I'll jot down how much you're betting when I have my break."

"Good stuff. I'll get back to tidying the shelves."

He wandered off, and Kit wondered what old-lady-dog combo she was going to be betting on come next Friday. Perhaps Mrs Morney and her sausage dog, since they clearly had two walks yesterday and might spring for three walks on a Friday. Especially if the weather was nice.

He and Kit had started a betting pool on which of the old dears walked their dogs the most. The ladies all ended up in the town's square at some point, which happened to be Greengage's gossip central and where a drinking fountain for dogs was placed. So, Kit, Rajesh, and Phyllis would saunter down there every Friday when the library was closed. They'd find a bench, place their bets, and then mark down the ladies strutting past with their adorable dogs. Phyllis might give them all a friendly bark, if she was awake and not snoring her wonky-toothed head off.

The trio would take walks around the square and buy teas and coffees during lulls, always keeping an eye on the dog walkers and the score sheet. The person with the losing bet had to bring a posh lunch for two to the library the next day. It wasn't scientifically laid out or a very sensible pastime, but then that was in the Greengage spirit. Besides, it gave the inactive Rajesh some more exercise and Kit something to do while Laura was working.

Suddenly, Rajesh waddled back toward her.

"Ah, forgot to ask how things went with the pretty Widow Caine? Had someone moved her books about, or was it all a load of old tosh?"

Kit slapped his arm lightly. "Don't say that. Of course it wasn't tosh!" She didn't mention that she herself had voiced doubts to Laura. After all, Laura had been right. Alice Caine was to be trusted until proven otherwise. Being friends with Rajesh had taught Kit not to count someone out due to them being over sixty.

"All right, Katherine. Keep your hair on!" Rajesh replied, as usual ignoring that no one else used Kit's full name.[1]

Kit stared into space. "Someone moved the books. Took one by Jules Verne, too. No clue why. I have my list of suspects, though."

"All right, let's hear it." Rajesh crossed his arms over his chest. "I can tell you the things about the suspects that Laura and Widow Caine will have been too polite to say."

"Okay. Widow—I mean, Alice said that she worried it might be her oldest, Phillip."

"Ah, yes. The man who gives the brave Royal Air Force a bad name. Stuck-up, strict, rude git. Why does she reckon it was him?"

"Firstly, he's often at her house borrowing books, especially lately. Laura hinted that he might be wanting to spend time away from his wife."

"I should think so. He and Jacqueline fight like cats and dogs."

"Secondly, Phillip is also the one who keeps protesting against investigating this bookshelf mystery, which is why

Alice worries he has something to hide. She says all her family think she's making it up and that she shouldn't tell anyone, but Phillip is apparently the most adamant."

"I bet he's the loudest about his opinions," Rajesh said with a grimace. "Greengage's proud RAF officer with a chip on his shoulder always thinks he's right and that everyone should listen to him, even if he has no clue what he's talking about. That might be why he keeps pushing this, because for once his mother won't obey him."

Kit pursed her lips and hummed. "Maybe. Laura hinted, in her polite way, that Phillip wasn't a pleasant bloke. Is that because of the constant back pain?"

"No, he's been boorish since he was a little nipper. Phyllis hates him."

Kit nodded gravely. Rajesh's lazy bulldog might not be good for much, but she did have a good sense for which people to avoid. "I see. Anyway, his wife is a suspect, too. Maybe he's covering for her? She had access to the key and knew about those few times Alice wouldn't be in."

"Jacqueline Caine? Ha! Good-looking woman, of course, and a flirt to boot. It caused quite a stir when Phillip married a woman nine years his younger." He gazed up at the paint flaking off the library ceiling. "They met when he was stationed in Scotland, I think. He brought her here and left her alone while he went back to the mainland and his Air Force duties. He came back once in a while to scold her for flirting with all the blokes. Oh, and to knock her up."

"Rajesh!"

He tore his gaze away from the ceiling and his reminiscences. "Fine, fine. 'To have children.' There, suit your sensitive ears better?"

"Yes. You should show some respect."

"Why? They don't respect anyone unless they're bloody aristocracy. Both Phillip and Jacqueline are middle class but like to pretend they're posh. Jacqueline once lectured me for half an hour for pronouncing Shostakovich wrong."

"Jackie," Kit said, using the nickname even though Rajesh wouldn't, "has seemed a bit guilt-ridden lately, Alice claims. But who knows if that has to do with the books."

"More likely to be about her array of lovers," Rajesh replied with an eye roll. "One of them being her brother-in-law, if rumours are to be believed."

"To be fair, Greengage has crazy rumours for everything. I mean, someone even spread a rumour that I was a witch because of my 'weirdly' blue eyes."

Rajesh grinned. "Ha! I fanned that rumour as much as I could. Said you won Laura over by putting a spell on her. Ruddy funny! The rumour about Anthony sleeping with Jacqueline probably has merit, though."

"How so?"

His gaze went back to the ceiling, as if that was where he stored memories these days. "Anthony Caine. Twitchy and tetchy bloke. Gossip says he lost his job as an architect because his ideas lacked imagination."

"Do you believe that?"

"Sure, Anthony is more ambitious than clever. He always wants more, he's never content. He was the same as a nipper. He got in trouble for stealing his brother's things and solved it by crying until everyone pitied him instead. That little weasel."

Kit clicked her tongue. "He's forty-nine and quite tall now, so he might be a weasel, but he isn't a little one. Well, no matter whom he sleeps with, he's got a key to Alice's house and knows her schedule."

"Right. So, who else could've gotten in to mess with the books?"

"Well, Alice thinks there's two other people with the opportunity."

"Let's be having 'em."

"The first is Liam Soames, the young bloke who lives next door and helps mow her lawn and do other odd jobs. He's apparently got a key to the back door so he can put tools and such away in the utility room when he's done," Kit said as she leaned against the library counter. "Alice says her family seems convinced he's only helping her so he can rob her one day."

"Yes, they would think that of a working-class lad who was thrown out of school," Rajesh grunted. "I remember the likes of them disapproved of my lower-class background almost as much as that I was an immigrant back in the day. Snobby bastards!"

"Mm. The prejudice towards Liam seems to have escalated now, since he's been out of work for quite a while and is openly struggling for cash." Kit tapped her lip, trying to remember who the remaining suspect was. "Oh, and of course there's Caitlin Caine, the granddaughter."

Rajesh shrugged. "Don't know much about her other than that she's Phillip and Jacqueline's smallest brat and rumoured to be as spoiled as her older brothers. I assume the others aren't suspects, since neither of them could stand to live in the same country as their parents?"

"No. They haven't been back to Britain for years. This business with the books has been in the works for about eleven months. It was at the kitten races last summer that Alice asked me if there was something strange about someone's books being moved about, remember?"

"Ah, yes. Why did she wait this long to ask you to actually look in to it?"

"Her sons kept telling her not to involve people. That it was probably Liam rooting around while looking for money, some friend borrowing books when she wasn't watching, or that she imagined it all."

"I see. What changed?"

"Last week I ran into Alice—"

Rajesh's bushy eyebrows shot up his forehead. "Surely you've seen her around during the past year?"

"Yes, but it was only last week, when I stood behind her in a really slow queue at the post office, that we got to talking and I got a chance to ask about whatever happened with the shuffled books."

"And?"

"She told me that nothing had changed since *Journey to the Centre of the Earth* disappeared, no more mysterious events but also no explanations. Despite this, her kids wouldn't let her ask around about it."

"So, she'd buried her head in the sand?"

"Well, as the books stopped being moved, she simply let the subject go and waited for the Jules Verne to pop up somewhere. Still, it seemed to really weigh on her when we spoke, so I convinced her to let me check into it."

Rajesh scratched his badly shaved chin. "Do you have any clue to why the book was taken? It's not even Verne's best work."

"Says you," Kit said while gently elbowing him. "And no, I don't know why."

"Hm. Was it a first edition or valuable in some other way?"

"Apparently not, no. I even asked Alice if there could've been anything important scribbled in the margins of the book or if it might have contained a note for someone. Anything out of the ordinary, really."

"And?"

"No, she says it was a common, unmarked, empty book as far as she knows."

Rajesh hummed. "And there were no signs of a break-in?"

"Nope. No one had been seen sneaking around either. There'd been no contractors with access to the house and no unusual guests. Laura was with me and asked about that twice. Still a negative."

"Does Widow Caine tend to leave her doors or windows open? Does she ever forget to lock the back door?"

Kit lifted an eyebrow. "I should ask you. You've dated her."

"Yes, but I was let in through the front door, Katherine," he admonished. "I don't tend to enter through ladies' back doors."

Kit suppressed the dirty double entendre which she couldn't allow her gutter mind to entertain. Smutty jokes didn't always go down so well on Greengage. She saved them for her best friend, Aimee. Sadly, that would have to be shared via phone as Aimee lived a ferry ride away, in Southampton on mainland Britain.

Rajesh sucked his teeth. "You know, there is another person who would've had a key to that cottage last summer."

"Really? Who?"

"Rachel."

This got Kit's attention. "What? Our Rachel?"

"If by 'our Rachel' you mean the lively, ginger pub owner who is best friends with your girlfriend, then yes."

Friends. Laura and Rachel had been a little more than friends back in the day. It was only due to Rachel's teenaged flirtation with her that Laura even suspected she might not be straight. It had taken falling in love with Kit last spring to cement that the well-known, well-loved heir to Gage Farm was bisexual—a series of events that had also been helped along by Rachel. The pub owner was a chatty, funny, extroverted sweetheart who was loved by everyone on Greengage. Surely she couldn't be a suspect?

"What does Rach have to do with this?" Kit asked.

"She's related to the Caines in some roundabout way. It's a small island, everyone is someone's second cousin or seventh aunt. Unless you're one of the rare people who were born somewhere else, like you or me."

"Okay, how does that make Rach a suspect?"

"I was getting to that, Katherine! She's not only related to Widow Caine, she also helps her out a bit. For example, Rachel cobbled together those big bookshelves that hold all of Widow Caine's books, with some advice over the phone from that hutch ladylove of hers."

"Butch, not hutch," Kit amended mechanically. She took her glasses off and rubbed the bridge of her nose.

So, Rachel built the bookshelves. This meant she had probably handled the books more than any of the suspects. That was a coincidence which was hard to ignore.

"The shelf building must've been a little before you moved here," Rajesh continued. "Rachel whinged for weeks about how hard it was to put the shelves up and how she knackered her back putting all the books in place."

"Hm. Well, I mean she wouldn't have a key to the

cottage for that," Kit argued. "She would do it when Alice was home. Besides, she could smuggle out the book then and there, no need to mess with the books later on, right?"

"No, I suppose not. She did have a key, though. Back then, Alice was helping Anthony the Weasel fetch some things from where he used to live. Stuff that had been with some ex, I think? She was with him as moral support for a day or two, so Rachel borrowed Liam's key."

"Why his key? Does she know Liam?"

"Oh, dear me, yes. Poor lad, everyone knows he has a bit of a crush on Rachel." He clicked his tongue. "Anyway, Rachel still pops by the cottage to help out once in a while, I believe. Changing light bulbs and such. The small stuff that Widow Caine wouldn't want to bother young Liam with."

Kit was itching to go talk to Rach about all of this. Never mind the other suspects, Kit's first stop would have to be Pub 42, the modern gourmet pub that Rachel and her long-term partner, Shannon, owned with the other gay couple of the island, Josh and Matt.

The third couple, Kit reminded herself. She and Laura were the first and foremost rainbow couple on the island as far as she was concerned, even if they were the newest.

Kit's thoughts were interrupted by a screechy, older voice saying, "Excuse me, miss. I am so sorry to bother you."

Detective work and workplace chitchat would have to wait. Kit slipped back into full librarian mode while Rajesh slunk away, probably to flirt with some of the ladies present.

Kit adjusted her glasses and smiled at the woman, whom she recognised as the grandmother of Laura's assistant. It was a small island, indeed.

110

"You're certainly not bothering me, madam. I'm here to help."

There was real relief on the woman's face. "Thank you. I have been searching for a book, using those clever computers of yours like Rajesh taught me, but they keep saying the title is on the shelf." She gave a grave shake of the head. "I'm afraid it's not, however. I've checked three times!"

"I'm sorry to hear that. Sometimes books do get misplaced. Or someone in the library might currently be reading it. I'll try to help you find it. What's the title?"

The lady leaned close to Kit, bringing a waft of herbal throat pastilles. "*A Guide to Better Orgasms for the Elderly.*"

Kit fought with every ounce of her librarian strength to not let any surprise be displayed on her face.

Control yourself. Better orgasms are a good thing to be searching for at any age. Besides, you have to be unfazed and professional!

Kit amped up her smile. "I see. That will be in the non-fiction part of the library then. Come—hrm, I mean, *follow* me, and we'll have a look together."

---

1. Experienced Greengage readers will know that Rajesh hates nicknames, meaning that Kit can't call him Raj, much to her disappointment.

Chapter Three

SHELVING ROMANCE AND THE TEDDY BEAR TECHNICIAN

I t would be a lie to say that Kit enjoyed her evening run. She missed the high-tech gyms back in London where she could be on a cross-trainer with her e-reader in front of her. Everyone around her would be wearing the same ridiculous breathable outfits and be equally sweaty. Instead, she was now out in public, pounding the uneven pavements while listening to an audiobook, which wasn't the same thing at all. Especially not as the narrator had just gotten to a tear-jerking scene where the main character's dog died. How was anyone meant to get in some good cardio while listening to that?

Kit stopped the audiobook and instead searched her phone for some music with a good beat. She nearly fell backwards, though, when she looked up and saw a big mass of auburn curls come hurtling toward her. Or, well, a person with said locks. Laura brushed the curls away from her face and tamed them into a ponytail. Her breath was shallow, and she had the wild-eyed look of someone who had forgotten their anniversary, left the oven on, *and* promised to give a presentation at work on a subject they knew nothing about.

"Dearest! Thank goodness I found you. I've been trying to ring you, but I know you miss calls when you're jogging."

Kit drew in a long breath so she wouldn't pant at her girlfriend. "Running, not jogging."

Laura waved her hand dismissively. "Yes, yes, whatever. I need to talk to you about my uncle."

"The recluse who lives with his equally reclusive adult kids in some sort of hut on the other side of the island?"

"The very same," she said, catching her breath. "Although, his recluse ways have faltered a bit. He has to go to London a couple of times a year, to check up on a business in which he is a silent partner. It seems last time he was there, he became involved with a teddy bear repair technician."

"He became involved with a what?"

"Do keep up, dearest. A teddy bear repair technician. Which isn't important right now," Laura announced, to Kit's disappointment. "What *is* important is that he dated this woman for about a week, at which time he found out that she was not only married, but that her husband was a former heavyweight boxer. A jealous one."

Kit whistled low. "Ah, all that'll put an instant stopper on any romance."

"Exactly. Uncle Maximillian hasn't had a partner since his late wife. Mainly due to his hatred of crowds and people in general, which means he rarely meets anyone. He is also rather… eccentric."

"Eccentric? By normal standards or by Greengage standards?"

Laura looked pained. "Both."

"Whoa."

"Exactly," Laura said. "He dropped in at the office a few minutes ago. I thought he wanted to check on Gage Farm, even though he isn't involved in the family business anymore, but what he actually wanted was to lament his failed relationship and say he needs a change."

"A change?" Try as she might, Kit couldn't figure out where this was going. All she had to go on was the nagging unease in her stomach, which felt like she'd eaten a kilo of vibrating marshmallow.

Laura avoided her gaze. "I'm afraid so. The change he has in mind is going back to the comfort of where he grew up, occupying one of the dusty guestrooms in Howard Hall. Oh, and remind me to thank my *helpful* cousins for this. They suggested that it might distract him to do a good deed for someone else, naming me as the prime victim—I mean, recipient."

"A good deed?"

"Yes. He decided that the act of charity will be advising me on how to run Gage Farm and shadowing me on a daily basis to see where improvements can be made. In short, he'll be glued to my side until his heartbreak heals."

"Okay. Wow. Yikes."

"Precisely."

"Sorry to hear that, babe. Not only because you'll be stuck with him but also because it sounds like he disapproves of how you're running Gage Farm. I mean, unless you really like him, his advice, and his company?"

Laura's full lips pressed into a thin line. "I've tried to like Uncle Maximillian my entire life. I'm ashamed to say I can't."

Kit almost reeled. "Have you got a fever or something? You always find the good in everyone."

"Yes, and there is good in him as well." She waved her hand in the air as if searching for examples. "He's interesting, well-meaning, and, um, well, he's harmless at least. He's also, as I said, eccentric. He can be selfish and highly strung, too," she admitted, looking pained to do so. "For example, if he has a broken heart and sees a happy relationship, he's likely to become disagreeable and impossible to be around."

"What do you mean?"

"After his wife died, whenever a family member or friend would display joy over being in love, he would give speeches about the injustice of the world and not stop until his throat got too sore to carry on." Laura looked heavenward. "He'd also sit and sigh loudly whenever there was a love song on the radio or someone mentioned romance or relationships."

"Well, I mean the guy was grieving, right?"

Laura gave her a weary glance. "This behaviour carried on for sixteen years after my aunt passed away. It's continued on, but on a smaller scale, ever since."

"Whoa. Okay." Kit ran a hand through her sweat-soaked hair and was grateful the night air wasn't cold. "Now, he's heartbroken again."

"Yes."

"And he's coming to stay with you?"

"Yes," Laura whispered this time.

Kit groaned. "Let me guess, you're going to do the sweet and dutiful thing and take him in even though you don't want to." She groaned even louder. "What's more, you're going to ask me if we can keep our relationship on the down-low for a while to stop him from making your life a misery every time we kiss each other."

Laura seemed to deflate with relief. "Exactly! I'm so glad I didn't have to explain all that. Kit, I know that'll be making you pay for the fact that I feel like I have a duty to the people around me, and I'm terribly sorry for that. I swear I will make it up to you. I just… I can't refuse him."

Kit sighed. "Fine. I won't have the argument about your sacrifices for others again. I'll play along until the old git feels better. I will, however, put my foot down if you tell me that I can't see you at all during the time he stays with you!"

"Oh, gosh no, I'll still see you," Laura quickly reassured her. "We'll only shelve the kissing and romancing for a while. I can't imagine not seeing you."

Kit tugged at a fistful of her sopping hair, as if this whole situation was to be blamed on it. Honestly, though, what could a mop of sweaty, short, black hair do against an irrational uncle and a girlfriend who always stepped up and helped?

Kit's mind went back to Christmas. It had been their first holiday season together, but several work emergencies at Gage Farm—as well as Greengage's events committee, which Laura chaired—had kept them apart for most of December.[1] That incident had taught Kit how to deal both with being away from Laura and with coping with her overly generous nature. Well. Sort of.

Kit accepted her fate and smiled at her girlfriend. "Well, we've been together for more than a year. I suppose we can do with some time apart—and some sneaking around—without joining your uncle in the lonely hearts club."

"I think so, too. Besides…" Laura's gaze flicked down

and then up again so that she was watching Kit from under the veil of her long, blackened eyelashes. "It might be fun to sneak around, stealing kisses and touches. We'll be like teenagers. Or forbidden lovers."

Just like that, Kit's heart began to pulse its appreciation for the doe-eyed seductress in front of her, a pulsing which soon echoed faintly between her thighs. "You're right, babe. As usual. Just don't let this go on for too long or let him take advantage of you, okay?"

Laura smiled. "I promise. I also promise that I'll make it up to you. How does a romantic holiday sound? And maybe some new lingerie?"

"For you to wear or me?"

"Whichever you prefer, dearest," Laura said, low and tempting.

"Then I'd like for you to wear it. Can it be mainly made of lace and quick to take off, please?"

Laura's sculpted brows shot up her forehead. "Well, I'm not going to say no to that." She paused. "Obviously, I'm never really comfortable with my body. However, I am *very* comfortable with how you react to it. Especially when it's in nice underwear. Besides, I quite like the idea of clothes being easy to get off."

There were so many naughty jokes about "getting off" and "being easy." However, Kit decided to keep away from more sex talk for the moment. She didn't want Laura to think that her only worry about them shelving their relationship for a while would be the lack of sex.

Instead, she smiled and said, "That's that sorted then. Was there anything else you wanted to chat about?"

"No, I don't think so."

"Alrighty then." Kit put her hands on her hips. "Are you going to join me for the rest of my run?"

"Yuck. Dearest, you know very well I only run if I'm being chased. Or someone's selling waffles with Häagen-Dazs on. With greengage jam. From Gage Farm, of course."

Kit rolled her eyes but knew from experience that Laura wasn't joking about happily sprinting for her favourite dessert. "Yeah, yeah, fine. So, I'll carry on running, and you…" She trailed off. "Hang on. Can we get back to what the hell a teddy bear repair technician is now?"

Laura rubbed one of those perfectly plucked eyebrows. "I believe it's someone who repairs damaged teddy bears. I don't know if she's employed by a toyshop chain or if she works only for serious teddy bear collectors and connoisseurs? You'll have to ask Uncle Maximillian."

"Ah, so I can meet him, then?"

"You'll have to if you're going to hang out at Howard Hall and have lunches with me and such. I think I'll introduce you as my best friend."

"Only for now, though, right? I've been out of the closet since I was a teenager and I don't fancy going back into it," she said, unable to keep from sounding as stern as she felt.

"Oh, dearest! No one is expecting you to go back into the closet. That's not why we're pretending to be just friends."

"I know."

"Do you? Because I need you to know without a doubt that I'd never hide the fact that I'm bisexual. Or that you're a lesbian." She took Kit's hand. "And I despise having to hide that I have the best girlfriend in the world. It's only to protect my uncle's broken heart."

Kit gave a reluctant smirk. "And your sanity while he lives with you."

"Yes, that, too," Laura said, shame making her slump. She stood right back up to add, "I'll tell Uncle Maximillian everything about us soon. I'll even explain why I felt the need to disguise our relationship and how badly that reflects on him."

"Yeah?"

"Absolutely! I'll tell him the moment he is either recovered from his heartbreak or at least ready to move out."

Kit stretched her left calf. Her legs were tightening up, and she needed to get moving again soon. "I just don't get how he can have missed what happened with Dylan, Sybil, and us. It was the talk of the island for months!"[2]

"He's a hermit, remember? He knows little of what's happening on Greengage. Or in the rest of the world for that matter. What's more, he doesn't care. Unlike Aunt Sybil, he has no concern for gossip about the Howards or for maintaining the family name."

Kit shrugged. "I guess that's why, then. Well, I should keep running before my legs seize up and my pulse drops too much."

Laura grabbed her waist with a possessive fervour and pulled her into a kiss, a long, intense one that made her toes curl.

When they broke apart, Laura whispered, "Or you can come home with me for a hot, steamy shower, so we can make the most of the time we have before my uncle moves in."

Kit hummed with pleasure. "Sounds like one hell of a great way to make sure my pulse doesn't drop. Lead the way to your car, love."

1. See the novella *Greengage Holiday Cheer*. Unless you're too busy, of course.
2. This unfolded in part one of the series, *Greengage Plots*. Best not to bore you with repetition. This story is long enough as it is, and we need to move on to more pressing things.

AUTHOR'S NOTE

Thanks for reading!

Greengage Shelf is coming to a bookstore near you in Summer 2019. Follow me on social media, or sign up to my newsletter via my website to find out more.

ABOUT THE AUTHOR

Emma Sterner-Radley, a Swedish romance and fantasy writer, got a degree in Library and Information Science because she wanted to work with books, and being an author was an impossible dream, right? Wrong. She's now a writer and a publisher. (But still a librarian at heart.)

She lives with her wife and two cats in England. There's no point in saying which city, as they move about once a year. She spends her time writing, reading, daydreaming, exercising, and watching whichever television show has the most lesbian/sapphic subtext at the time.

Her weaknesses are coffee, sugary snacks and small chubby creatures with tiny legs.

www.emmasternerradley.com

ALSO BY EMMA STERNER-RADLEY

LIFE PUSHES YOU ALONG

Zoe's on autopilot. Rebecca is stagnating. When change comes knocking, will they open the door?

Twenty-something Zoe Achidi feels safe in her unchallenging life in a London bookshop. Bored, but safe.

Her only excitement comes from pining over frequent customer, Rebecca Clare, unobtainable as this beautiful businesswoman in her forties seems.

One day, Zoe's brother and her best friend bring Zoe and Rebecca together.

While they connect, and it turns out Rebecca is also bored with her life, their meetings remain all business. When things take a turn for the worse, life pushes along.

But will Zoe and Rebecca end up being thrust in the same direction?

If you're looking for an age-gap romance that will inspire you to shake up your life, then look no further.

Take the leap with Life Pushes You Along by Emma Sterner-Radley

LIFE PUSHES YOU ALONG | PREVIEW
by Emma Sterner-Radley

CHAPTER ONE

Zoe watched as one of her favourite customers observed her with what seemed to be desperation. She felt her heart twinge with sympathy.

"So, do you have it?" he asked.

She knew she was going to disappoint him.

"I'm not sure, Mr. Evans. A book with a bird on the cover that was based somewhere with a big forest... that doesn't ring a bell, I'm afraid."

The bookshop's unpleasantly sharp fluorescent lights showed every crease on his wrinkled face as it took on an embarrassed look.

Zoe quickly added, "I know the feeling though. There's lots of books I have been looking for and I can't remember anything but the cover, or a piece of the plot, or half of the author's name. It's a pain."

He nodded. "Yes. Yes, my dear, it certainly is."

"Do you remember anything else about the book? Who was the main character?"

He looked up at the ceiling for a moment. "I suppose she was quite a bit like you, actually."

Zoe felt her brow furrowing. She didn't want to be rude but that didn't narrow it down much. Did he, perhaps, mean that the main character was someone who worked with customers, someone who dressed like her, or someone who was in their late twenties? She hoped he wasn't alluding to the fact that she wasn't white because she wasn't sure if a conversation with this elderly gentleman would stay politically correct if they got onto that subject. She liked Mr. Evans and wanted to continue liking him.

"I see. Um, how was she like me?"

"Young and likable," he answered simply.

Zoe was relieved. It was still just as impossible to find the book he was looking for, though.

"I'm afraid that doesn't give me much to go on. Tell you what, I'll keep an eye out for a book with a forest setting and a bird on the cover. We have your contact details on file, so I can call you if we get it in?"

His face lit up. "That would be splendid! Thank you ever so much for your help."

She smiled at him, happy to be able to help. Mr. Evans put his trilby hat back on, and she couldn't help but smile at his posh, old-fashioned sense of style which perfectly matched his way of speaking.

"Goodbye. I hope to hear from you but if I do not, I shall come in to purchase another book instead."

"You do that, Mr. Evans. Goodbye."

Just as he was leaving the bookshop, he turned around and shouted, "Oh, by the way, it might have been something other than a bird, now that I think about it. I think it was something that flew. So, maybe t'was a bat, a moth, or perhaps a ferret? Anyway, cheerio."

The door closed behind him and Zoe stared into space, puzzled.

Had he meant to say 'ferret'? How the hell was that categorized as something that flew?

Zoe's manager, and the owner of the bookshop, Darren, walked in with a small box under one arm.

He held out the box to her. "We've got a book delivery. Who was that?" He inclined his head towards the door.

"Oh, it was Mr. Evans."

Darren's bushy eyebrows met at the bridge of his nose. "Who?"

"Mr. Evans. You know, the retired bank manager who likes books about nature and sea journeys. Comes in here every week?"

Darren still looked like he was trying to do complicated arithmetic.

Zoe managed not to sigh. "The old guy with the big mole on his right cheek?"

"Oh, that crazy, posh old badger. Right. Anyway, here's the new batch. Put them on the system and then shelve them, will you?"

She gave a curt nod and took the box from him. There was no reason why he couldn't do this himself–well there was one reason and that was simply that he was lazy. He'd stand at the counter and watch her put the books out, and as soon as she was done he'd slink back into the breakroom, leaving her to man the counter as always, while he drank his bodyweight in sweet tea. *No wonder he always needs to use the loo*, she thought as she unpacked the books.

She put them on the system and looked at the packing slip to check the details as she did so.

Her job wasn't the dream that most other book-nerds conjured up when she told them what she did. Yes, she worked in an independent bookshop. However, it was a lacklustre bookshop, where she was overworked, her boss didn't care much about the running of the place, and the clientele was dwindling.

As Zoe began to shelve the books, she looked around at the cheap birch bookcases, faded beige walls, and harsh fluorescent lights and thought about how she had ended up here.

She had been in dire straits when she applied for this job. She had been out on the street since her parents kicked her out. She didn't think she was focused enough for further education, she was down to her last twenty pounds and totally unqualified for any job.

Out of desperation, she had applied for this position and when Darren had asked her, in the interview, why he should hire her and not the other two applicants, who both had degrees and experience, she had broken down in tears. He had grumbled about not being able to stand seeing people cry and after a long chat about her situation, he had agreed to give her the job on a trial basis. She had never known how to thank him for that, and so she merely put up with him as a way of showing her gratitude.

She had just turned eighteen back then and she had stayed in the job for the following eight years out of loyalty, habit, and a feeling that there was no other job out there for her.

She sighed as she placed another book on the shelf. What was she qualified to do? Other bookshops were run a lot more professionally than Darren's Book Nook. Her quick foray into wanted-ads told her that they would demand that she "showed initiative" and "managed her own workload." She was sure she wasn't ready for that. She figured that a trained monkey could do the job she was doing right now and so that was what she would stick with, no matter how much it bored her.

The little bell above the door rang out. Before Zoe had time to turn to see who their new customer was, she heard Darren's sharp intake of breath. She knew immediately who must be at the door. Rebecca Clare.

Their favourite customer was shaking drops of water from her elegant brown coat and looked unfairly beautiful despite her red hair being wet and her glasses covered in little raindrops. Zoe stole as many glances as she dared while Rebecca rid herself of the worst of the rain. She admired the fancy high-heeled shoes, the black stockings, and what she could see of the knee-length black dress under her coat. And that was saying nothing about her face; those stunning eyes and the heart-shaped lips were truly mesmerizing. Especially this close up. Rebecca was near enough for Zoe to be able to reach out and brush her cheek. Not that she was daydreaming about that, of course.

Zoe knew she shouldn't be staring. Not only because it was rude, and borderline objectifying, but because Rebecca was way out of her league. And far too old for her. Zoe didn't know how old Rebecca was but she was certainly older than her own twenty-six years. Oh, and to make Rebecca even more of an impossible choice, she was Darren's huge crush too.

Just as Zoe was dragging her gaze away, she saw Rebecca quickly remove her drenched glasses. The water that had rested on them shot out in Zoe's direction, some hitting the side of her face.

Rebecca looked mortified. "Oh, I'm so sorry. Are you all right, there?"

"Yeah, sure! I'm, uh, waterproof," Zoe replied. She hoped her tone was light and jokey but worried that she sounded as terrified as she always felt when this woman spoke to her.

They had never had any long conversations, she realised. Zoe, and by extension, Darren, only knew Rebecca's name because she had ordered books and they always took contact information to be able to call or e-mail the customer when their book arrived.

Rebecca Clare, RebeccaClare@acacia-recruitment.com, Zoe repeated in her head, stopping herself before she reeled off the memorized phone number too.

The contact information, which showed that she must work in recruitment considering the company's name, and Rebecca's fondness for crime-fiction was all Zoe knew about this woman. Well, that and the fact that she had the sort of presence that you couldn't miss. Despite Rebecca's feminine looks and apparel, there was almost a masculine air to her behaviour. Zoe realised that what she saw as masculine could probably be boiled down to confidence, calm, directness, and a sense of power. Rebecca was polite and friendly but in a way that spoke of a person who you couldn't take for granted.

Either way, Rebecca Clare demanded all the attention of her onlookers without having to fight for it. And that, combined with her obvious beauty, took Zoe's breath away. Just as it was doing right now as she stood with droplets of water running down her cheek and Rebecca smiling politely at her.

Zoe wiped away the water from her face with her sweater sleeve and watched Rebecca dry her glasses on a tissue she had taken out of her pocket. Then she put the glasses back on. Zoe struggled to find something to say. Something normal. Something witty.

She heard Darren clear his throat and come rushing over.

"Mrs. Clare, isn't it? Come to pick up your latest bloodcurdling chiller?" He grinned at Rebecca. Zoe realised that he probably thought it was a charming smirk. It wasn't.

"It's *Ms.* Clare," Rebecca replied casually. "And yes, please. I got an email a few days ago and haven't had time to pop in until today."

"Terrible weather for it, though. You should have waited until tomorrow," Darren said, his strange smile still fixed in place.

Zoe saw Rebecca raise an eyebrow for a brief moment.

"Well, it's meant to rain all week, so planning to only go out when it's dry seems futile. We're Londoners, right? We're experts at dealing with rain."

Darren laughed, far too loudly and for far too long. Zoe wondered if Rebecca was suffering from second-hand embarrassment as much as she was right now. Deciding to rescue the other woman, Zoe put the books down and went behind the counter to pick up the book Rebecca had ordered and put it through the till.

When she was done, she handed Rebecca the thick tome. "Here's your book. I've never heard of this author. Is she any good?"

"Very good. Or, at least, her last three books have been. Here's hoping her latest doesn't disappoint." Rebecca looked down at the book and gave the front cover a quick pat. Then she looked back up at Zoe, with a smile.

Zoe felt herself freeze. She was meant to be telling Rebecca the total for the book, and asking if she wanted a bag but all she could do was stare. The charming smile was bad enough but Zoe had just ignored her own advice – never look this woman in the eye.

Rebecca Clare's eyes were a common blue-green colour, but what made them so dangerous was that they always seemed to glimmer. As if Rebecca was constantly happy. Or constantly flirting. It was insanely distracting and Zoe had to force herself to ignore those gorgeous eyes and just say the total sum. She barely remembered to offer a bag for the book.

When Rebecca had paid and thanked her, she turned on her high heels and click-clacked back out into the rain and out of Zoe's line of vision. Zoe sighed deeply and stopped herself when she realised that Darren could probably hear her.

It turned out that she didn't need to worry about that. Darren was busy staring after Rebecca, looking like an abandoned puppy. Zoe looked around at the shop which suddenly looked ten times duller and knew how he felt.

Published by Heartsome Publishing
Staffordshire
United Kingdom

First Heartsome edition: June 2019

45422754R00087

Printed in Poland
by Amazon Fulfillment
Poland Sp. z o.o., Wrocław